DRAGONS, Inc.

D. D. McDee

HUGO HOUSE PUBLISHERS, LTD.

ISBN: 978-1-948261-67-8

Library of Congress Control Number: 2022907103

Cover Illustrator: Izmalov Alexander

Cover layout, page design and interior formatting:

Ronda Taylor, www.heartworkcreative.com

Hugo House Publishers, Ltd.
Austin, TX • Denver, CO
www.HugoHousePublishers.com

Introduction

Dragons like me. I'm not really sure why, and when I ask them I get very enigmatic answers, mostly along the lines of "We like you because we like you." I have the idea they like me in the same way a human likes a puppy. It's weird being considered a pet, but since I like them too, it all works out.

So, since I know a few dragons, I thought it wouldn't be a bad idea to let others in on some dragon facts as well as a few stories about them. They really are very interesting companions. I hope you meet one someday. You'll never be the same again.

CHAPTER 1

Guardians of the Skies

J was sitting on a boulder on the side of a mountain, overlooking a beautifully serene valley. It was very relaxing, right up to the point where fire bloomed all around me. It shifted and flowed in a warm, ever-changing display, but didn't burn. I jumped but did not scream, as this had happened more times than I cared to remember. I sighed and tried to look stern as I turned to look at the dragon who is my best friend.

"Geez Larry, do you have to scare the crap out of me *every* time you see me?", I asked.

"Of course I do. It's funny.", said Larry.

I growled. I do know that isn't a proper method of expressing myself, but I did it nonetheless. I put it down to spending too much time with dragons and too little with people. "To you maybe.", I said.

Larry laughed, *"Oh come on, admit it. You find it funny as well."*

Much as I did not want to admit it, it was true. Larry's ability to sneak up on me so easily was as entertaining as it was mystifying. After all, he's about thirty feet long, has a wingspan of about forty more feet, and his feet are huge with really long claws. I had asked him a half a dozen times how he could so easily sneak up on me, and the only answer I ever got was, "magic." It suddenly dawned on me that maybe I'd been asking the wrong question.

You see, Larry (like all dragons) could teach a Zen master lessons in being cryptic. In fact, I think they did teach the original Zen masters, but that's just my suspicion. I've never been able to get a straight answer from Larry on that particular subject either.

One of the things that made it so easy for Larry to sneak up on me was that he didn't smell like what I thought a dragon should smell like. Here we were in the mountains where I had gone for a nice relaxing hike. Even with Larry there, all I could smell was pine and fresh air. Larry didn't smell like anything at all.

I felt like an idiot. How did I not notice this before? The thing he most didn't smell like was fire. How could this be? He'd just shot out enough fire to set the forest ablaze had he aimed it at the trees, but no smell.

"Hey Larry. How come you don't smell like fire, dude?"

Larry smiled. *"You just now noticed?"*

I rolled my eyes but did smile back. "Well, what's the answer? And if you say magic, I'll scream."

"But that is the answer." After my scream, Larry continued, *"Here, I'll show you."* Larry leaned back his head and shot a plume of fire into the air. He was careful, as this was fire season and the last thing we needed was more mountain fires. I could feel the heat of it, but there was no smell whatsoever.

"The fire's magic?"

"Yep. How else do you think I can breathe it without hurting myself? It is fire, and it does come out of my mouth."

I was truly amazed. "That's just awesome. Can you turn it different colors?"

"Sure." Larry demonstrated with a fire show that made fireworks look positively mundane.

Before I could quiz him more on the various aspects of magical fire, Larry plopped on the ground, sighed, and laid his head on the boulder on which I was perched. Another big sigh followed. These were wind-tunnel sighs. Sighs to make the angels duck. Sighs that could blow the paint off a Ford.

"What's up Larry? I thought you were going to a Renaissance festival this weekend."

"I was going to, but it just seemed so boring. I'm bored."

I looked at Larry in alarm, and the more I looked, the more my concern grew. He looked droopy and his scales were dull—not a good sign. Larry's scales were usually a bright iridescent blue which means they also threw off rainbows of color in the sunlight.

Dragons are immune to almost everything except wizards, other dragons, and their own boredom. The wizards and dragons had opted for a cease fire a long time ago, so that wasn't currently a problem, but dragons did disappear. Those who weren't killed in the war didn't die; but they did disappear if they got too bored. None of the other dragons could ever find them again. None of them had ever returned.

It usually took a few decades between the onset of dragon ennui to the disappearance phase, but once the boredom set in it was hard to drive away. As I said, this was a problem.

When I first met Larry about ten years ago, he had just started to feel the ennui. For some reason, meeting me had pulled him out of it, but if it was starting again, I had to help him. I was quite happy that Larry found me entertaining, and I fully intended to keep it that way because he was not only fascinating, he was also fun.

But what do you do to keep a creature who is over a thousand years old interested in life? I thought about it for a while and then inspiration struck. I spun around on the rock, put my hands on either side of Larry's huge snout, and shared my great idea.

"What you need Larry, is a job!"

"What?!"

"A job. You know, something you do to keep from being bored!" He looked appalled but that was better than bored, so I decided to make my case. "Look, studies have shown that lots and lots of humans die shortly after retiring from their jobs. So, by extrapolation, having a job might make life worth living. We need to figure out a good job for you and maybe even your friends."

"Ahhh, you're worried about me." I swear if he had hands Larry would've patted me on the head.

"You bet I am. I like you Larry. I want to keep you around."

Larry smiled and curled his humongous tail around me in a sort of dragon hug. It was comforting and frightening at the same time. Dragon scales are hard and sharp.

"You're so cute."

I tell you, it's pretty weird being a dragon's pet and that was certainly how Larry seemed to think of me.

"I've never had a job. What kind of job do you think I could do?" Larry's tone was both amused and skeptical. *"And it has to be something I do, not just arrive and be in a parade or a decoration at the entrance to a renaissance fair."*

"How about movies? People are interested in dragons again. There are all kinds of movies with dragons in them. You could save producers millions in special-effects fees." I stopped talking as Larry contemplated the possibilities.

"Okay, what do we do?"

"I don't know. I guess I need to do some research. I'll meet you back here tomorrow."

"Deal."

The next twenty-four hours were a nightmare. Having determined that the first action for any new or aspiring actor was to get an agent, I spent hours and hours trying to find one for my friend. You try wading through rabid receptionists to get to an agent and then explaining to them that you needed them to represent a dragon.

They wouldn't even talk to me. Several times I was pretty sure that if I'd been in their office, they would have called the funny farm and had me taken away.

With laughter from a dozen agents ringing in my ears and my fingers sore from dialing so many numbers, I changed tactics. I looked up all the recent movies and television shows that featured dragons. I researched the people involved. Producers, directors, anyone I could find. I printed off their pictures. Larry and I could figure this out, I was sure we could.

The next day when I met Larry, he was actually looking much better. His scales had a bit more of the iridescence that marked a healthy dragon.

"Okay Larry, we have to get a bit creative. If I show you pictures of certain people, do you think you could find them?"

"Probably, if you give me some idea of where to start. Once I know who they are, I can find them at will."

"Really, that's interesting. How does that work?"

"Everyone has a sort of psychic signature. It's like a personal wave length but on a much finer scale. Once I meet someone, I can look for that signature using magic, and find them in a heartbeat. That's how I always know where you are."

"Hmmm. I actually kind of understand that. It's sort of another sense. Like the feeling I get when I know someone is watching me even though I can't see them. Like that?"

"Yes."

"You always know where I am?"

"Yes."

"That's kind of cool." I contemplated that for a moment and decided I'd think about it later because it started to give me the creeps. "Okay, let's get started." I showed Larry pictures of the producers and directors I had googled. Rather than show the pictures directly to Larry (they were really tiny even though I had printed out 8x10s of each) I carefully studied each one while he looked into my mind. It tickled a bit, and although it was slightly unsettling, it wasn't too bad.

"So, here's what you do Larry. Find those guys, then this weekend we'll see if we can waylay a few of them and offer your services."

"You got it boss." Larry disappeared and I drove back to the city to do some of my own work. I am a game designer, so I can set my own hours. I bet you can't guess what my games feature. Or maybe you can...

When the weekend rolled around, I met Larry outside the city, and we got started. One of the directors was going fishing for the weekend and we decided to start with him. Since he would not be surrounded by crowds of people, theoretically making contact with him should have been a fairly easy thing. Larry and I went to the lake and waited until he was far away from the shore in his boat. I figured since he couldn't run away, we would have him as a captive audience. Then I had Larry do a Nessie imitation by keeping the majority of his body underwater and only showing his snout and part of his back. Well, we definitely got the director's attention. He and the actor who was fishing with him were busily taking photos of Larry as he came closer and closer.

When Larry rose up out of the lake next to the boat, I truly wasn't expecting them to freak out. Being in pictures, I thought the director and his friend would figure it was some sort of special effect and at least tried to figure out how it worked. I thought wrong! You would think that people who spend their lives creating fantasy worlds on film might be a little bit more open minded about fantastical creatures. Don't these guys have any imagination? Suffice it to say that the answer to that little question is a resounding, "NO."

It took me an hour to calm him and his fishing buddy down. When I finally did, they were so amazed at seeing a real live dragon that it took me another two hours to get their attention so I could explain why we were here. Then the wheels started to crank.

They were starting a new movie project that did involve dragons (which I knew from the internet) and would be delighted to have Larry's services.

A month later we headed off to Hollywood and found out how movies were made.

The day we reported to the set was one of the most entertaining days of my life. The director and producer, who had been clued in to the new "actor" for the movie, had gathered the entire cast and crew in the field where they were planning to shoot a number of the dragon scenes. The director asked that we come in and land near where everyone was gathered, so we did.

The gamut of reactions ranged from sheer terror through stunned disbelief to wild enthusiasm. As soon as I dismounted, I was swarmed by prop guys who started peering and poking and prodding to figure out just how I had put this astonishing "prop" together. Larry let them explore for about two minutes and then put a stop to it by rearing back and snorting a plume of smoke from his nostrils.

The prop guys were undaunted. The head guy came over to me as his compatriots were inspecting Larry's claws and scales. "Hello. My name is Robert."

"I'm Deanne, and this great beast is Larry."

He laughed, "Wow, you named it Larry?"

"No actually, he named himself."

Robert laughed.

"No, seriously, he did."

I happened to glance over as one of the prop guys was trying to pry up one of Larry's scales. "Hey you! I wouldn't do that if I were you. You might piss him off." The amused chuckles that greeted my warning were abruptly cut off when Larry grabbed the guy, picked him up, held him at eye level and shook his head in the universal "NO" gesture. The guy looked Larry right in the eye, realized that there wasn't a prop in the world this good, and promptly apologized.

"Your apology is accepted." While many of those circled around didn't hear Larry's words, many did.

For some reason the director couldn't hear Larry until the last week. I don't know if he was just too caught up in his own world or what. I didn't worry about it too much, as I was getting a nice big fat fee for being Larry's coach. I was even acknowledged in the credits of the movie as the "Dragon Wrangler," much to my amusement. Larry got a pretty good kick out of it too.

"CUT!" the director shouted. He then turned to me, "Hey Dragon Lady. Can you get the dragon to come on over here? I have some directions for him."

I resisted the urge to slap him. I have a name, so does Larry. And really, shouldn't he be showing a bit of respect to a creature that was not only saving him bucket loads of money but was pretty amazing to boot? I called Larry over, and he landed right in front of the director.

My friend Larry is one of the mellowest persons I had ever met. However, I could tell that the director was starting to get to him.

The director looked at Larry and asked, "Could you try to fly a bit more majestically?"

I looked at Larry, and he looked at me. Even though his face never changed, in my head I heard, *Can you believe this guy?*

I put on my best poker face and said, "He says he can try." Unfortunately the director wasn't done.

"Can you have him make the fire a little more intimidating?"

I suppressed the urge to laugh. "I'm pretty sure he could." I turned to Larry. "How about it? Could you make the fire a little more intimidating?"

Larry had obviously had just about enough. "*I can do that.*" Larry launched himself into the sky, flew over the little pond next to where we were filming and let forth a stream of fire that was so hot, bits of what looked like lava dripped from the flames. He boiled the pond in about five seconds flat. Great clouds of steam lit orange by the fire rose into the sky. Larry then flew through the steam and gently landed in front of the director. "*Like that?*"

The director actually heard Larry's voice that time and didn't miss the dripping sarcasm. He paled and nodded. "Yes that would be just fine. Thank you." We even got footage of Larry's temper tantrum because one of the cameramen had been waiting for Larry to do something unusual. When I spoke with the cameraman after, he said he could tell things were about to go south when he saw the fire in Larry's eyes, so he filmed it all. They even used it in the movie.

After that, things went much smoother. More than a few of the actors and support people came up and thanked me later. Apparently the director was more than little hard to get along with, and they were delighted that Larry had knocked a bit of the arrogance out of him.

I was more than a little relieved that our portion of the movie only took a month to film. I swear, the magic that appears on the screen is just plain hard work in the trenches. I met more prima donnas, drama queens, and just plain unpleasant people than I ever wanted to meet in an entire lifetime. While we met some truly delightful people, there were plenty of others who thought that the universe revolved around them. And really, when you're working with a real-life dragon, who is the most important person (or creature) on the set?

Once we finished that particular project, we both agreed that this was not the job for Larry. On the bright side, I was delighted to see that he was now in the spirit of the whole "Let's find a good job for Larry" project. His scales were practically glowing, and his interest was definitely back.

Larry's rise in interest continued over the next couple of weeks. Although he got more engaged, I myself experienced a few heart-stopping moments.

The first incident was when I was walking back to my car from the symphony. My car was only a few blocks from the concert hall, so I wasn't really worried about walking back to it after the show. I said goodbye to my friends and set off. As I turned the corner, I met some very unsavory types. There were three of them, and they had those overdone scowls and that "hip" bad attitude that assured me that they were up to no good.

Even as I experienced a spurt of fear, I had the presence of mind to shoot out a sort of mental 911 call to my friend. Larry let me know he would be there in a jiffy. Yes, he did send *jiffy*. Larry loves slang. Did I mention that he's a really young dragon, only a little over a thousand years old?

"Hey, you," the first one growled, "give me your purse." If I hadn't known that help was on the way, I really would have been frightened, but as it was, I found myself calming down. In fact help arrived just as the lead guy was growling out his demand. Larry landed quietly on top of the building behind me. The miscreants were so intent on their thievery that they didn't even notice.

The guy doing the talking seemed like a bad imitation of a thug. He wasn't even handsomely broody or anything.

Knowing Larry was just above me gave me courage. "No, you can't have my purse"

I could tell by the startled look on his face that this was the last thing he expected. Pushing my advantage I continued, "And I think you should just call it quits, go home, and have your dad buy you some pizza or something."

Let me tell you. That was definitely the wrong thing to say. He went off like a nuclear bomb. Spit showered me as he yelled, "Give me your purse, or I'll kill you." There were more words after that, but I'm not going to repeat them. Some people have so little imagination. Curse words featured almost exclusively in his tirade. Thankfully he was more intent on intimidating me than in doing me physical harm.

I looked at him very calmly and said, "That's probably not the best idea you've had this year."

The guy was more than a little confused. "What are you talking about? You're crazy!"

I didn't say another word. I just pointed to where Larry had landed. There he sat with his wings spread out to their full extent and just a little smoke curling out of his left nostril. Just to complete the effect, he hurled a little fire at a dumpster, which glowed red as the contents burst into flames.

Have you ever seen a tough-guy wannabe faint? It's a sight to behold. The other two probably broke Olympic records getting out of there. They looked like the roadrunner in the old Saturday morning cartoons.

I started laughing and couldn't stop for about ten minutes. My sides hurt. My eyes were watering. I couldn't breathe properly. I was gasping for air.

Larry laughed as hard as I did. His laugh was a kind of rolling rumble and small bits of multi-colored fire escaped as he did so. "Man-o-man Larry. Those guys thought they were so bad. You really took them down a notch. The look on the leader's face was priceless. Maybe they might think twice before bothering someone else."

"They'll probably decide it was the drugs they were taking."

"You're kind of cynical, my friend."

"Well, you're a little naïve."

"That may be, but just because I hope for the best doesn't mean that I'm not surprised when it doesn't come out that way. I guess I'm just a cynical optimist."

"No, you're just an optimist. You always think the best of people. You always have hope for things getting better."

"And what's wrong with that?"

Larry didn't say anything for a very long time. *"Nothing really. It might be an interesting way to live. I might try it for a while just to see what happens.*"

"Well in the meantime, how about we put out this dumpster fire and call it a night?"

Larry looked at me quizzically, "*How? I just start fires; I've never put them out.*"

"Seriously?"

"*Yeah.*"

It didn't take us long to figure out how to get the fire out (Larry smothered it with his wing), and we took off just as we heard the fire-truck sirens. It was definitely an interesting ending to a night out.

The next incident occurred when I was flying to Los Angeles. One of the gaming companies I work with was having some difficulty with one of my games, so I was flying in to sort it out. Normally when I want to go somewhere, I just go with Larry. He is much faster than any airline, but the company was sending someone to meet me at the airport and explaining Larry as a mode of transportation was just a bit much. Easier to take a plane, I thought.

Man, did I pick the *wrong* flight. One of the engines caught fire at thirty-thousand feet about halfway into the fight. I thought the championship game when the Broncos beat the New England Patriots was loud. That was positively polite compared to the panicked screaming I heard that day.

I silently sent out a call to my friend. He arrived instantaneously. He was barraged by all the thoughts that were running through everyone's heads—mostly "Oh My God I Don't Want TO DIE." He cut through the cacophony and asked me what he could do. I didn't really know, so I told him to see what the pilots were thinking.

The plane was still in the air. It was listing but wasn't plunging towards the ground, so the sounds around me abated somewhat. It made it easier to concentrate on what Larry was telling me.

The "fasten your seatbelts" sign came on with an announcement that the pilot had activated it along with verbal instructions for everyone to fasten them. Duh!!!

Apparently, the pilot was keeping the plane in the air but needed to know what kind of damage there was to the wing. Larry could see the entire wing, but didn't know enough about airplanes to assess what damage was critical and what didn't matter. He needed more data from the pilots.

"So Larry, just ask them."

"I'm trying. They don't hear me. Not many people listen to dragons. They just dismiss us as odd voices in their heads."

"Okay, I'll take care of it." I unbuckled my seatbelt and ran for the front of the plane. I was seated in the first row and the attendant was near the back of the plane checking everyone's seat belts, so he wasn't quick enough to stop me. I got to the locked door of the cockpit and grabbed the phone to the pilot.

"I can help you find out the status of the wing if you'll let me in."

The pilot was well versed in terrorist tricks so didn't open the door. He did, however, ask me what I was talking about.

I sent a message to Larry to fly up towards the front of the plane, which he did. I then instructed the pilot to look out the window. "My friend there can find out what you need to know, but he has to relay it through me because he says you can't hear him."

You have to love pilots. When they are sitting on that line between life and death, they don't waste a lot of time asking stupid questions like, "Is that what I think it is?" The pilot was obviously willing to believe his own senses. There was a short silence and just before the flight attendant arrived to drag me away, the door clicked open, and I slipped in.

I was relieved to see that the pilot looked old enough to be my father. That meant he had probably handled more emergencies than I had ever imagined. He reassured the flight attendant who had called him on the same phone to make sure everything was okay then turned to me.

I pointed out the window at my friend and said, "Larry says that you need to know how much damage the wing has sustained. If you'll tell me what you need to know, I'll get him to look. It would be easier if he didn't have to go invisible again, so if you could get the passengers to shut their window shades so he can work without being seen, we can figure this out."

The pilot dutifully got on the intercom system to instruct the passengers to close their window shades. His bogus, want-to-protect-you-all-from-any-flying-debris explanation worked. It's amazing what people will believe when they're terrified. We got on with it as soon as the shades were drawn.

The pilots asked about rips in the metal covering the wings. They had Larry check to see if there was any damage to the underlying structure, if anything was leaking, etc.

Larry checked everything out and cheerfully reported back. When they were trying to determine just what was dripping out of the plane's wing, Larry even tasted it to find out. Good thing he's got an iron stomach because what he was tasting was apparently hydraulic fluid mixed with jet fuel. He told me he'd tasted worse, which was just odd.

As Larry was doing his flying diagnostic, the pilots were bringing the plane down to a lower altitude, radioing in their emergency, and trying to find a landing field that they could reach. There was no good news in any of this. With the fuel leaks, we wouldn't be able to make it to an airport with a sufficiently long landing field. The wing was damaged in such a way that the flaps wouldn't work and there were several rips in the wing that were widening. This would make landing more like crashing. I'm not very fond of crashing, so I thought as quickly as I could.

"I have an idea. Let's see if Larry can grab onto the plane and just fly us down or glide us down using his wings." I knew we were going to get to the ground one way or the other, but I really wanted to walk away from this one.

The pilot frowned and asked, "Do you think he can hold up that much weight?"

Larry heard the question and replied, *"Sure, I can do that. This plane is a toy compared to some of the things I have flown with."*

I just looked at them and shrugged, "Well he says he can."

The co-pilot looked incredulous and shook his head. "How is that possible?"

I laughed and raised my hands palms up in a dramatic gesture. "He's a dragon. He's flying over five-hundred miles per hour. He's been eating jet fuel and hydraulic fluid with no adverse effect. I don't know how any of that's possible. But if he says he can do something, he probably can."

The pilot smiled, "After this is over, I really want to talk to the both of you."

"Okay."

Larry grabbed the damaged wing and used his own wings to help guide the plane to the ground. After getting us down safely he promptly disappeared before any of the passengers got a glimpse of him. There were some witnesses who thought they saw some sort of creature wrapped around the plane, but the reports were generally put down to hallucinations due to smoke inhalation.

I gave the pilot, David, my number and expected that to be the end of it, but I was incorrect. I got a call two days later.

"Hello. This is David, the pilot on your flight."

I smiled. He just sounded so friendly. "Hello David. What can I do for you?"

"Actually, I called for two reasons. First off, I'd like to know what you and your dragon friend would like for saving all of us. If he wasn't a dragon, I'd take you out to dinner, give you a reward, and free flights for life. But I'm pretty sure your friend would like to keep a low profile, and I'm pretty sure he doesn't need any plane tickets. So, I was wondering if there's something he really likes that I could give him. Got any ideas?"

I thought for just a moment. "Well, he really likes gold, but he's got lots of that. His favorite things are chocolate, beer, and country music."

There was a long silence on the phone. I could tell that David was trying to figure out if I was jerking his chain or not. "Hmmm. I would never have guessed that." He thought for just a bit, and I could hear him muttering to himself, "I could call Bob, who knows Melinda who works for the Grand Ole Opry House ... yeah, this could work." Then to me he said, "Can I call you back in a couple of days?"

"Sure." I was sincerely intrigued by what he was planning. He hung up and I realized that I didn't know what the second thing was that he wanted to talk to me about. Oh well, I'd just have to find out in a couple of days.

Sure enough, David called me back two days later. He sounded excited, which is saying something because I have found that most pilots are the least excitable people I have ever met. They seem to take in anything with a dreadful calm that I can never seem to emulate. "What are you and your dragon doing tonight?"

"I don't know. What do you have in mind?"

"A surprise. Can the two of you meet me at Redrocks Amphitheater tonight at 7:00 p.m.?"

"You bet. Will Larry like it?"

David laughed, "He's gonna love it."

I called Larry and he agreed to pick me up just before seven. For those of you who have never been to Denver, Red Rocks Amphitheater is a natural rock formation of sandstone—red of course—that has been turned into a theater. It is nestled in the foothills west of town and rock concerts, plays, graduations and other events are held there regularly. There is a spectacular view of Denver from the higher seats. It is one of my favorite places to go to concerts because the acoustics are amazing, and the setting is peaceful.

Larry and I arrived at just before seven, and David and several other people were waiting for us by the stage. Other than them, the park was deserted. There were big signs and the police were keeping people out. We saw them as we flew over.

I had neglected to introduce Larry to David on the day my plane went down, so I rectified that immediately. The other people with him were the flight crew of the plane Larry had saved. Introductions were made all around. They all gave him hugs and thanks, which I thought was pretty brave of them. Then David asked him to find a comfortable place to settle in. Once we did, David had a giant vat of beer and several carts of chocolate of all kinds rolled over where he presented them to Larry. Larry's scales shimmered as he looked at this largess. He was actually really surprised that all this was being done for him. He even had me tell everyone they could help him eat the chocolates, and we all did.

Then the lights came on and out came Home Free, one of Larry's favorite groups. They sang all of Larry's favorite songs. Larry slurped up the beer, munched on the chocolates (which the flight crew happily unwrapped for him) and even got to meet all the guys in the group, which really topped off the night. I have never seen Larry happier.

When it was all over, David came over and sat with us. I told him how much Larry really liked his reward. David smiled and said, "That's the perfect lead in for the second thing I'd like to talk to you about. When our plane had trouble, Larry was there almost instantaneously. I assume that means he can do that anytime, correct?"

I nodded.

"Well, I'd like to hire him as a sort of guardian dragon for the airline industry. If we could figure out a way to alert him in a true emergency, no one would ever have to die in a plane crash again."

Larry was very interested. *"Does this mean that people would know about us again?"*

David looked a bit chagrined, "Well some people would have to know, but we could keep it somewhat quiet if that's what you want."

I was delighted to note that David could now hear Larry. As I learned on the movie set, all it really takes is a willingness to listen and anyone can talk to the dragons. I didn't want to be Larry's only friend in the human community, so the more people who could hear him the better in my mind.

Larry overheard my thoughts, *"I am getting more and more friends thanks to you. I am so glad you are my best friend!"*

I smiled and wiped a tear from my eye, "Same goes." He had used a very private thought that no one else could hear.

He then got back to David, *"I'll have to check with the other dragons as this affects us all."*

I thought David was going to have a heart attack right then and there. "There are more of you?!"

"Yes."

"How many?" David asked. I myself had never been able to drum up the intestinal fortitude to ask Larry this question.

"Fifteen of us are left."

Neither David nor I knew what to say. When you're talking dragons, fifteen is both a lot and at the same time a very small amount. I asked the next obvious question, "How many did there used to be?"

Larry just looked sad. *"Before I was born there were tens of thousands. No other dragons have been born since me."*

"So that means you're the littlest dragon. That's awesome." I turned back to David, "Thanks David for a wonderful evening. We'll get back to you after he talks to the others."

The dragons had their conclave. I heard they hadn't had one for about three hundred years.

They decided they would like to be guardian dragons. They even wanted to learn about airplanes. With that, Dragon Aviation Services was born. The dragons worked out a schedule. David and his friends worked out a sort of dragon signal which they had installed in every airplane in the world (using some of the dragons' gold), and the skies quickly became safer than ever.

The hardest part about the whole thing was figuring out how to pay the dragons. Between them, they have more gold and gems than all the countries in the world combined. We asked them repeatedly what they would like for being our guardians. The answer was all about them not being bored. So we built a giant movie theatre and made sure there were enough drinks and snacks for all the dragons. Even though they don't have to eat, they really like snacks. We show them whatever movies they want. All fifteen of them show up every week. They seem particularly fond of stupid comedies. Would you believe it? Dragons love The Three Stooges. It's painful, it really is.

We also hold concerts for them of all different kinds of music. Other than Home Free, none of the performers know who is listening, as we tell them that the audience is made up of reclusive millionaires who don't want to be seen. The performers get paid pretty well, so they don't ask all that many questions. We have a screen that allows the dragons to see in, but the musicians can't see out. We've even done a few plays. The dragons are not bored.

The best part of the whole thing for me was that I got to meet all the other dragons. They are a very interesting group.

So now a few more people know about the dragons. It's not a problem, but sometimes I still worry about it. Not that humans can harm the dragons, but people can be weird. I don't know what they would do if they knew about my friends.

So we help people, and we stay out of sight. The dragons feel useful. I guess helping others really is the way to a richer life. Well, at least that's what the dragons think, and I tend to agree.

CHAPTER 2

The Business of Dragons

You have no idea how many businesses have to be started to care for such a small group of dragons. First there was Dragon Aviation Services to protect the airlines. Then there was Dragon Entertainment Industries to build the movie theatre and rent the movies, get the popcorn and drinks, etc. for the Dragon's entertainment. It's a really big theatre. Fifteen dragons take up a lot of space.

Then there was Dragon Antiquities, Inc., the company we started to sell off some of the dragon gold to fund the other enterprises. The dragons had coins that were so old and in such good shape that antique dealers were darn near wetting their pants when we showed up. We had to be careful to put only small amounts onto the market at any one time so as not to crash the antiquities markets. Then, to explain how these things appeared in the first place, we had to open Dragon Treasure Explorations.

I had to buy boats, jeeps, and all-terrain vehicles (which is great fun when you have unlimited funds), hire people, buy dive equipment, and on and on and on. This was so that they could go and "find" all these lost treasures.

Oh, and I *had* to test drive all of the above, at least that's what I told everyone. The dragons really loved it though. They got to figure out places to hide the gold that would make it hard to find, then we'd plant rumors for treasure hunters to chase down. We funded their explorations for a portion of the find.

We actually used Dragon Treasure Explorations as a way to boost the economy of some very poor places. We'd find some area that needed a serious boost, then we'd start rumors about treasure in the vicinity. Then our guys (and other treasure hunters as well) would go to that place and spend lots of money on food, lodging, and locals to act as guides. We'd then put together these great brochures when the treasure was "found" about the area, and tourism would definitely pick up.

As things started rolling, I had to build a headquarters for everything. It had to have entrances for the dragons and hallways wide enough for them to navigate. Well, I didn't build it myself but you get the idea. Lots and lots of new projects every day.

The only real downside of this was the paperwork. Each business generated mounds of paperwork, paperwork that could keep a small army of secretaries busy. And this was all generated regularly. Did I mention that I really truly hate paperwork?

I was sitting at my desk doing paperwork, and bitching about it in my head, when Mildred appeared. Sometimes I thought maybe I shouldn't have made an office the size of a small hanger so my dragon friends could pop in whenever they wanted. But since I was doing paperwork, this was not one of those times. I cheerfully put down my pen and looked up.

Mildred didn't look so good. She looked positively gloomy.

"What can I do for you Mildred?"

"We want you to start showing movies or TV every night."

"Why."

"Well, we're still pretty bored."

"What about your job helping the airlines?"

"It's great and all, but I only work one day a week. And there're hardly ever any emergencies. I'm not unhappy about that, it's just not very exciting" She looked at me with big droopy eyes. Her size sort of ruined the "poor me" affect, but I did appreciate the effort. *"So, can you open up the theatre every night?"*

"No." I absolutely refused to turn the only remaining dragons on Earth into couch potatoes. That would just be wrong. Mildred knew exactly what I was thinking.

"How about four nights a week? That wouldn't turn us into sofa tubers."

"Two!"

"Deal." Mildred smiled. *"So, I guess you need to find me another job or something to do for the rest of the time."*

"Hey, I do not recall being made the Entertainment Director for all the dragons on Cruise-ship Earth."

Mildred just looked at me. The droopy eyes were gone. She was starting to look fierce. Dragons are actually pretty scary when they get mad. "Okay, Okay," I said. "Don't get your tail in a twist." Mildred just looked at me. I thought my "tail in a twist" comment sounded pretty good, but Mildred completely missed the reference. I guess converting human slang into dragon slang isn't my strong suit except with Larry who seems to get it right away.

I grabbed a legal pad and pen from my desk drawer and did my best super secretary imitation – all formality and false perkiness. "Okay Mildred, what skills do you have?"

"Skills?"

"Yeah, skills. Employers need to know what your skills are."

"Well, I can fly." I dutifully wrote that down. *"I can breathe fire."*

"Got that." I wrote that down as well. "Anything else?"

"I'm really strong." I wrote that down as well.

"Anything else?" I waited patiently – at least that's how I tried to look. This whole thing was pretty foolish in my mind.

"No, I guess that's about it."

"Okay. Got any people skills?"

"What do you mean by people skills?"

"Things like, 'good at customer service,' 'good at handling disputes,' that kind of thing."

"No, no people skills."

"All right. Now what kind of a job would you like?"

"I don't know. What kind of jobs are there?"

"Well, let's look." I grabbed my computer and pulled up Craig's List. "Hmmm. Jobs for dragons. MILDRED, THERE ARE NO JOBS LISTED FOR DRAGONS!"

Mildred looked a bit taken aback, *"You're a bit testy today."*

I rolled my eyes, "It must be the paperwork." She just sat and looked at me. Since I knew it was no use trying to win a staring contest with a dragon, I gave in. "Okay, let me tackle this a different way. What do you like, Mildred?"

Mildred thought about it for quite a while. *"I like fish. I like whales—they are really cool. I like swimming. I like to be helpful. I like jewelry ..."*

At that point I sort of tuned Mildred out as an idea started to swirl through my head. After I caught it with my mental butterfly net, I tuned back in.

"... I like stars. I like the taste of chocolate. I like fireworks."

"Okay stop. I have an idea. I'll call you when I have it worked out."

It took me almost a week, but I finally had it all arranged. I called Mildred, and we met her potential employer on a very out-of-the-way beach. We'll call him Mr. Smith for confidentiality reasons. He had no idea that the applicant was a dragon. I had her land behind a large group of rocks and asked her to stay there while I walked out to the beach to meet him.

"Why all the secrecy?" he asked.

"Well, my friend really does want to help the whole environmental cause. She truly loves whales, but she's a bit controversial."

He laughed, "We do controversial."

I just raised my eyebrows and smiled. "We'll see."

At that point I whistled and Mildred jumped up over the rocks she had been hiding behind and sailed low and slow over to where we stood. Mr. Smith's eyes almost popped out of his head as his jaw dropped and he started backing up. The closer she got the further his jaw dropped. He backed up right into the water and just kept going. He didn't stop until he was about ten feet out at which point he couldn't seem to settle on whether he wanted to stare, try to swim away, or what.

He kept rubbing his eyes and looking at Mildred. He didn't even seem to notice the waves crashing around his legs. Aliens could have landed to the sound of trumpets, and he probably wouldn't have noticed. He kept pointing and saying, "Is that a…a…That's a…No, that couldn't be a …" He couldn't seem to get the word dragon to come out of his mouth. I was wondering if there would be a complete sentence anywhere in my future, but it didn't seem that one would be coming anytime soon.

I shrugged eloquently, hands turned up and out in a "what's the big whoop" sort of gesture. "Hey dude, don't you appreciate the delicious irony of a really, really endangered species helping you to save other endangered species?"

He stopped stuttering and somehow managed a complete sentence. "How - how can he help?"

"First off, he is a she. Mildred, I'd like you to meet Mr. Smith."

She merely stopped next to me and dipped her head in a greeting. Mr. Smith started navigating back through the water toward her. He was shaking head to toe, but he kept coming. I had to admire his pluck.

"As for how she can help," I continued, "There are lots of ways. She's freakishly strong, and she could pick up any beached whale or dolphin and put them back into deeper water in a heartbeat."

He stepped a bit closer and took a good look at her claws. "Without hurting them?"

"Yes, without hurting them. She can be really gentle when she wants. She even has a pet poodle."

He came closer yet. I don't think the poodle comment even registered. Mildred really loved that stupid dog. I have to admit, I was pretty fond of him as well.

"And another thing, you wouldn't have to put your ships at risk. Can you imagine any whaler ignoring a warning from her?"

"Uh...no." He finally made it out of the water and slowly looked up.

"And if they don't get the message immediately, she can breathe fire!" Mildred did so. I thought he was going to pee himself. Actually, he may have done just that, but his pants were already wet from the water so I couldn't be sure.

He finally looked her in the eye. "So, you want to help us?"

"Yes, I do. I like whales."

His smile was slow to start, but his mouth sported a great wide grin at the finish. "I do too." He stood there for a full minute just smiling and shaking his head. I was a bit surprised to see the smile suddenly drop away. "Hey," he asked Mildred, "what am I going to pay you?"

Mildred looked at me expectantly. I threw out my hands in frustration. "What? Am I supposed to know all the answers?"

Mildred continued to look at me expectantly. Mildred is the master of making you talk by just looking at you. "Fine. Mildred, what do you think would be good pay for helping these guys save the whales?"

"Jewelry. Pretty, pretty jewelry. Humans have all kinds of nice jewelry. We just have the jewels. I'd love to be able to wear them."

We both looked at Mr. Smith who looked very perplexed. "I don't know where to get Dragon jewelry."

Mildred looked crestfallen. I snorted. "Of course not. There isn't any such thing. You have to figure it out. Don't you have someone in your organization who might be able to make some jewelry on a very, very large scale?"

"Hmmm. I just might. It might be a bit expensive to make though."

"Don't worry about the money. We have plenty, and if you have people who can make jewelry, we can set them up in business and they can make it for the other dragons as well. I suspect they would all like to get in on this one." As a note, we ended up hiring blacksmiths to work with the jewelers to make amazing dragon jewelry. They loved it.

Even as the words escaped from my mouth, I was cursing myself inwardly for starting yet another business. Just what I needed, more paperwork. I really needed some help.

I ended up hiring a tremendous personal assistant and an entire flock of super-secretaries who do the paperwork. It took them a while to figure out that they were setting up businesses for dragons. Well my personal assistant knew, but the others were mostly kept in the dark, at least for a while, but they eventually caught up. It became a sort of company joke. The old hands that knew what we were doing would take bets about how long it would take one of the newer employees to catch on while dropping hints that were so obvious that only the fact that "everyone knew" that dragons aren't real kept the new guys from picking up on the hints sooner. When they finally did realize what was really going on, there was always a big party, attended of course by one of the dragons or several of them, depending on the day. Most of the dragons loved parties. For creatures that had been out of sight for so many years, they really were quite sociable.

When the reports of a dragon protecting whales hit the internet everyone thought it was a clever photo-shopped hoax. I was a bit worried at first, but decided to just leave it be. After all, the dragons were helping people. Who in the world would object to that?

Next up was Harley. He was one of the older dragons. I was setting up the movie theatre one night when he cornered me. *"Can I talk to you?"*

"Sure Harley, what's up?"

"I want to do something useful." He then sighed loud enough to startle birds out of trees in the next county. I'm telling you. Dragons really have that sighing thing down to an art form.

I wanted to sigh myself and bemoan my fate. Thinking up jobs for dragons isn't the easiest thing in the world, but really, like the Queen in *Through the Looking Glass*, I did like thinking up impossible things, so it always worked out.

I made an appointment for Harley to come see me the next day in the office, then finished setting up the movie for the night. We both enjoyed the movie along with our friends. As the night drew to a close, I wondered what I would do for Harley the next day.

I hadn't spoken with Harley much, so I was a bit nervous when he arrived. The older dragons were very intimidating for a number of reasons. For one thing, they were much larger than my friend Larry. They had also survived the times when the wizards and the dragons had been at war, and I was never sure if they had truly gotten over it. After all, my people had killed quite a few of theirs. Of course, it went the other way as well, but none of the humans involved were still alive. The older dragons were, but since it was a very long time ago, we had a sort of don't ask, don't tell arrangement. Even so, I did find them a bit frightening. I tried to keep my thoughts to myself, but of course that didn't really work.

The first thing Harley said was, *"Worry not little girl. We're not the same dragons as we were, and you are certainly not the one who attacked us."*

I sighed with relief. "Thanks Harley. I have to say you're a lot more forgiving than I might be in your shoes." Harley merely bowed his head. "Now, let's find out what kind of a job you'd be good at."

I started asking him many of the same questions I had asked Mildred, but without the sarcasm. He interrupted me pretty quickly.

"I've been talking with Hexley, and he's really enjoying his work with the children." Hexley was the first dragon I had met when I was a teenager. He loves to be read to, and he gets children to read to him wherever he goes.

I chuckled, "Wow, he's still doing that?"

"*Yes, he is. Apparently, the children love him. He says it is one of the most surprising and joyful things he has ever experienced. I have to say, that is an intriguing concept for me. I can't remember a time when someone loved me. I would like something where I could have a sort of human family so to speak. I would like to be loved.*"

I blinked back tears and continued. "Okay, let me think about that one. I'll get back to you." After Harley left, I actually broke down and sobbed. Imagine living for thousands of years and not feeling loved. Well, that was going to change and right now! I spent the entire night researching, thinking, coming up with ideas and rejecting them before I finally settled on a solution.

The next day when Harley came back, I was all prepared. "Harley, I have an idea. All night I kept coming back to your basic abilities— breathing fire and being able to fly. That plus your incredible strength gave me an interesting idea. I'm thinking that we could go to one of the poorer countries that have villages high up in the mountains. Some of these places have brutal winters, and very little infrastructure. If a place like that had geothermal energy to tap into, or in your case dragon-thermal energy, to power things as well as heat things, it would make all the difference in the world. They could set up greenhouses and grow food in the winter, and they could add tourism to the mix with hot springs. That along with the capability of getting supplies in easily and any produced goods out, and it's very possible that the people of the village could turn their attention to something other than bare survival. If that were the case who knows what might happen."

Harley mulled it over for quite a while. He finally looked up. *"Okay, how do we find a village?"*

"We could do flyovers of the areas I am thinking of and just see if we see one that needs help. Of course, it also has to be a place where you'd be willing to live."

Harley was most definitely in. It took us two weeks, and I got to see some of the most beautiful mountains in the world from a vantage point no one else has ever had--on the back of a dragon. It was awfully cold, but well worth it.

We went to Tibet, Peru, Mongolia, Nepal, China, the Appalachians, and Africa. Harley settled on a small, almost inaccessible village in Nepal, where a recent earthquake had devastated the town. Half the buildings looked like they would fall down if you dared to sneeze, and the people looked just as broken as their homes.

We landed in a field at the edge of town and just waited. Harley's really good at waiting. Me, not so much.

In Nepal dragons are traditionally held in high regard. However, a theoretical dragon and a real one are worlds apart in the overall scheme of things. I was pretty impressed that it didn't take very long for the people of the town to come investigate. What brave people these were. I was even more impressed that they had gathered several baskets of flowers as a gift for Harley. Where in the world had they found flowers in the midst of all that devastation?

I don't speak Nepalese, so I couldn't follow the entire conversation between the town elders and my friend, but I got the gist. They were delighted to have Harley come join their community and could certainly use his help. As soon as Harley told me they were planning to throw him a party, I called Larry (mentally of course) and had him bring along some food, well actually a lot of food. The village was preparing to use what little they had to welcome their new friend, and I thought we should contribute as well.

As they were preparing the feast, I saw one little girl walk up to Harley and throw her arms as far as she could around his face, which really wasn't that far. I had to wipe the tears away once again as I saw Harley's reaction when she followed the hug with a kiss, right on his snout. He couldn't have been more stunned or more pleased. I could tell that he was going to love his new job. It's great when you find the right job for the right dragon.

Harley's doing great, and the village is thriving. With Harley's help they cleared the rubble, started building, put up greenhouses and bath houses and made the place shine. It is now a major tourist destination, and everyone thinks the local legend about a dragon who saved the town is very quaint. Not too many people know it's true.

Several weeks later Larry and I were lounging by the outdoor pool at the Dragon Enterprises main compound when Melissa suddenly appeared. Of all the dragons I think Mel is the most beautiful. She's coal black, but with an underlying iridescence that ripples across her scales like flowing water whenever she moves. The tips of her wings and some of her scales are lined in a brilliant gold. She headed straight for Larry and me. After landing she gave me a pitiful look and said, *"Hey, we could really use your help."*

I could hear the underlying (attempted) con as soon as I heard her voice in my head. She wanted something that I was pretty sure I wasn't going to like—whatever it was. I replied suspiciously, "What's going on Mel?"

"Well, Doug and Pete –"

I cut her off immediately. "I don't even want to know. I'm serious. I am not responsible for those two reprobates. I don't even want to know what they're up to. If they're doing something they shouldn't be, you guys have to handle it. I'll find you all jobs, I'll play you movies, I'll even arrange live entertainment, but I refuse to be the Police Chief for bad boy dragons. Really."

Mel thought about it for a bit. "*I see your point. We will take care of today, but you really have to find them jobs. Maybe that'll keep them out of trouble.*"

"I doubt it, but I'll give it a shot. Send 'em over tomorrow, and I'll see what I can do."

Mel nodded and leapt into the sky. Larry looked at me and asked, "*You really don't want to know?*"

"No, I really don't. They are *not* my monkeys, and I am *not* the Ring Master for their particular circus!" Larry just chuckled.

When Pete and Doug arrived the next day, I just looked at them and shook my head. "So, what do you guys think you should be doing?"

The two of them looked at each other. Looked at me. Looked at each other. Looked at me. Tilted their heads like a couple of innocent puppies, and in unison thought, *"We don't know. What do you think we should do?"*

"I don't know. You guys seem to be driving the other dragons crazy. They think if you had a job, you'd be happier and would cause less trouble."

Doug's head came up instantly. *"We don't cause any trouble!"*

"Really? Who accidentally flooded an entire valley because you were having a contest to see who could melt the most snow in the shortest amount of time?"

They both looked a bit sheepish. Doug offered his very best justification, *"We did dry it out."*

"Yeah, with fire!"

Pete replied, *"We only lost a couple of trees."* I just glared at him, and he shut up. Doug wisely said nothing.

"And who scared the crap out of the space shuttle guys with some flaming lightshow?"

Silence.

"And who has been appearing and disappearing and flitting by aircraft thus making people think that aliens are flying around in our skies?"

Doug rested his head on my desk and sighed, blowing all the papers off the desk and onto the floor. *"Well, that would be us."*

"My point exactly," I said, ignoring the mess he had just made of my office. "You two need something useful to do." When they both agreed, I did my standard dragon job interview on them and then kicked them out so I could think. I couldn't think of a single thing these two could do that didn't involve mayhem. So I decided to turn my mind off and brainlessly cruise some silly videos on the internet. I ran across a really cool video for Japanese beer where a couple of dragons were helping to make it. I wondered if that might actually work. I knew Doug and Pete both liked beer, so maybe making it would be right up their alley.

I called them back in, and they agreed instantly. I contacted Sapporo (the Japanese beer maker) and asked them if they wanted actual dragons to help make their beer. They did. They also wanted to use them in commercials. Filming live dragons is a lot cheaper than CG dragons. So now, Doug and Pete are making beer and beer commercials and staying out of trouble. Well mostly. If you want to see the commercial just go to YouTube and type in *FULL Sapporo Premium Beer Commercial Legendary Biru.*

I have to admit that the best job the dragons have is one they got themselves. I was puttering around in one of the gardens at our compound when I was descended upon by five of my dragon friends. Joan seemed to be in charge.

"What's up guys?" I asked.

"There is a big fire headed toward this town up in the mountains, and we would like to help. But we don't know how." Joan said.

"That's a challenge alright," I said as I tried to wrap my wits around how creatures whose greatest ability was causing fires could possibly put one out.

I thought about it for about five minutes, and then realized that since I didn't really know how to put out fires, any ideas I came up with would probably be lame at best. I looked at Joan and asked, "Can you find where the firefighters are gathering for directions and such?"

"Sure."

"Then let's go. We'll ask them how they could use you to help. Tell you what. Rather than all five of you showing up at once, why don't we do this? Joan and I will go talk to whoever is in charge while the rest of you scope out the fire, and we'll call you when they get over their inevitable freak out."

The dragons chuckled and agreed to my plan.

When Joan started circling down to where the firefighters were gathered in their field headquarters, people scattered like leaves before a leaf blower. We landed, and I jumped off and yelled, "Who's in charge here?"

A very angry man came striding over, "I am, and I don't really have time for whatever this is."

Joan looked at him, cocked her head and told me, *"There's a crew trapped up on the mountain and he can't get his helicopters off the ground because of the winds. He's very worried. He thinks they might get burned or even die."*

I strode over to meet him halfway, put my hands on my hips and said, "We can help. Dragons can fly in any weather, and they're immune to fire. We can go get your guys."

He shook his head. "It must be the smoke. I think I'm hallucinating," he muttered to himself.

"You're not," I replied emphatically. "Can you give me a few firefighters to ride the dragons to explain to your guys that they should come with us?"

He looked at his men who had drifted closer. One of them had even ventured to reach out and touch Joan. "Any volunteers?" he asked.

Several brave souls raised their hands, so I called the other dragons. Everybody moved back again to give them room to land. I assigned dragons to the volunteers who could hear them, and we prepared to go. Even though he was pretty sure he was out of his mind, the Captain made me suit up in fireproof gear before I left. As his men cautiously climbed aboard the other dragons, I joined Joan, and we headed out.

"You do know where they are, right?" I asked Joan.

She snorted, *"Of course!"*

As we flew in, I could see that the flames had completely surrounded a small group of men and women. The firefighters were shaking out what looked like blankets as the flames moved closer. I later found out that these were special blankets that were supposed to protect them from the flames as the fire came closer. However, with a fire that hot, it was possible that they wouldn't have survived.

The embers were swirling around like angry fireflies as we landed in between the closest fire and the firefighters. I jumped down and started shouting, "Get on the dragons! We'll get you out." Unfortunately they too thought they were hallucinating and just stood there staring until their fellow firefighters jumped down and basically dragged them over to the dragons. We all mounted up and flew back to the field headquarters.

After everyone was done slapping each other's' backs and cheering, I went back over to where the Captain stood. "So Captain, how else can we help?"

The Captain walked over to where Joan was standing. He walked all the way around her, inspecting every part of her. He then turned to me and started peppering me with questions.

"Can they carry heavy loads?"

"Yes."

"How heavy?"

"I don't know for sure, but quite a bit."

"Can they really breathe fire?"

"You bet."

"Do you think they could carry large fire buckets?"

"Yep. They'll need someone to release it when they get over the fire."

"We can do that. I only have three buckets available, and I see you have five dragons. Let's rig up the three, while I send some guys to go get more buckets."

"We can go get them. I'm sure we're faster than a truck."

"Okay," the Captain agreed.

"Maybe you should go with us. I don't think they would cheerfully hand over equipment to a strange woman on a dragon."

He smiled wryly, "Good point. Let's go."

By the time we returned from getting more buckets, three of the dragons were dumping loads of water on the fire. The firefighters were directing them as to where to dump it and then releasing the catches on the buckets. The dragons would then disappear, and after a short time reappear with another full bucket and repeat. Mike, the dragon who hadn't had a bucket, was standing there with his head cocked watching the proceedings. Apparently he'd had some time to think while listening to the firefighter's thoughts. When we landed, he looked at me and said, *"I have an idea how to get the fire put out faster."*

"Okay, go for it."

Mike put out a call to the other dragons and they divested themselves of their equipment. They asked that the firefighters stay on board to help them make decisions. Joan asked me to come along, and Mike had the firefighter he had worked with before mount up. We all rose into the air and followed Mike.

Boy was I surprised at where we ended up. We arrived above Iceberg Alley. For those of you that don't know, Iceberg Alley is a portion of the Atlantic where icebergs travel in the spring and summer. Below us was a beautiful parade of icebergs. The dragons each picked an iceberg they thought they could lift and rose into the air with giant chunks of ice in their talons. They popped back to where the fire was and asked the firefighters to let them know where to put them down. After a number of trips, they had a wall formed on the leading edge of the fire so that it wouldn't spread. They then got geared back up with the buckets, and dumped more water on the fire itself.

It took several days, but they got the fire under control, saved the town, and made tons of friends. This was the event that made people very, very aware that there were still dragons living on Earth. It was great that the reintroduction was all about how the dragons saved not only a group of firefighters, but an entire town as well.

The town was so grateful that they have set aside a weekend every year to celebrate the dragons saving them. They called it Dragon Days, and invited all the dragons to come back every year. I'm pretty sure they will.

So, anyway, I still have a few dragons that need jobs, so if you have any great ideas just contact Dragon Enterprises, Inc.

CHAPTER 3

Dragon Land

There I was happily (and this is written in the most facetious way) doing paperwork in my office when I felt a slight breeze come my way. I looked up and saw a serious looking young man standing in my office door. I had no idea how he had gotten past my assistant, but I saw no harm in being friendly. It's sort of my default mode—at least until you purposely provoke me.

"Hello. How may I help you?"

He scowled as he fairly growled his answer, "You can help me by ceasing and desisting with all these dragon activities. They're dangerous. They can be vicious. Who knows what they'll do? The council is very, very unhappy." He then turned away with a flourish and disappeared in a flash of light.

I started laughing. I couldn't help it. It was so over the top. So dramatic. Sooo serious. I had the thought that the only thing that would have made it more like an actual melodrama was a cape. He forgot his cape. Oh well. It was a good effort anyway.

Then I started wondering, "Who was this guy and what council was he referring to?" I wasn't too worried. Bad acting aside, he hadn't seemed dangerous, just a bit odd. Best of all, he had given me a good laugh and a break from my paperwork. Rejuvenated, I got back to it and the rest of the paperwork went much quicker.

Later that evening I asked Larry about my experience, and he said, *"Oh, he's talking about the Wizard's Council."*

"Wizard's council? There's a wizard's council? Who are they? What do they do? I thought wizards were ancient history. Are they the same wizards? Do they live a really long time like you do?"

"STOP!" Larry shouted. In a more reasonable tone, he continued, *"I can only answer one question at a time. Yes, there are wizards. Yes, they are really old. Yes, they have a council. No, none of the wizards still alive were 'those wizards'—the ones responsible for the slaughter of the dragons. There is a particular type of magic needed to kill dragons, and there are no more wizards alive that know that magic."*

I was so relieved. For just a moment I'd been a little concerned for my friends. After all, they are a really endangered species. None of the dragons liked to talk about the wars, but I had managed to get a few answers to my questions before this conversation with Larry. But his next statement shocked me, for I incorrectly assumed from Larry's answers that after wiping out most of the dragon population, the wizards responsible eventually passed away.

Larry looked at me and in that instant I saw a deep, deep anger that I had never seen in any of the dragons. *"No, they didn't die off. We killed them."*

"We as in you?" I blurted the question out even though I didn't really want to know the answer.

"No, I was too young. If you really want to know what happened, I could introduce you to Li Chen. He was there."

"There's a wizard that's over a thousand years old? Wow!"

"There are several, but I think Li is the oldest."

"So, does this Li Chen guy run the council?"

"No. He doesn't like politics."

"Well, that's an interesting twist. How do we make an appointment to go see him?" Suddenly I wanted to know everything, and at the same time I didn't want to upset my friends by asking them. But I had no problem asking a complete stranger. Since this Li Chen guy was probably involved, I figured I'd take his information with a grain of salt, but I could ask him questions, and boy was I going to take advantage of that.

Larry paused for a moment then said, *"He says we can come over now if that is convenient."*

"Hmmm. I thought we'd have to wait."

"No, he's heard about you and wants to meet you."

"Okay. That's not intimidating at all."

Larry just laughed. *"Come on chicken girl. Let's go."*

With a name like Li Chen, I thought that maybe we were going to go to China or Japan. But really, when you're over a thousand years old and you are a wizard, I guess you can live anywhere you like. China isn't really the paradise the Communist Party would have you believe, so Mr. Chen lives in Wyoming, which is great, because it's pretty close to Colorado, which is where I live.

As we sailed in from above, I decided that I really liked Mr. Chen's taste. His house was a log home (not a cabin) that boasted loads of windows to see the views. But at the same time, it didn't look like one of the eyesore mansions people insist on building in beautiful mountain territory. It was nestled up against a cliff with a wide-open area that was surrounded by trees, so from a distance it didn't stand out much at all. It also had a really big swimming pool and what looked like a coy pond. I love those weird fish. *"So do I."* Larry chimed in.

Mr. Chen was standing in his back yard when we landed. He smiled at Larry, "Hello, my friend."

"Hello back, my friend," Larry responded. *"Deanne, Li. Li, Deanne."*

I walked over and reached out my hand. I had been expecting a small, wizened old Asian guy. That's not what I saw. I saw a thirtyish , handsome, willowy, tall Asian guy dressed in jeans and a t-shirt. He must have detected my surprise. "Not what you expected, eh?"

I smiled, "No, not really. I expected you to look really old."

He laughed. At that moment I noticed that Larry had wandered over to the swimming pool and was blowing multi-colored fire under the water. I sighed, excused myself and went over to where he was. "Larry. Larry! Hey, LARRY!" I smacked him as I yelled both out loud and telepathically. He finally pulled his head out of the water and looked at me.

"What?" His expression was the epitome of innocence.

"If you want to play in someone's swimming pool, it is good manners to ask first."

"*Oh. Sorry. I didn't know. Hey Li, can I play in your pool?*"

Li shrugged as he raised his hands in a gesture of puzzled acquiescence. "Absolutely. Be my guest."

I walked back over to where Li stood. He kept looking back and forth between Larry and me. "Did you just school a dragon on proper human manners?"

"Yes. We've been working on it. All the dragons are getting much more polite."

"I see." Li paused and then gestured to a table and several chairs positioned on the beautiful pine porch. "Care to join me in some refreshment?"

"I would. Thank you." We walked over to where he had iced lemonade, cheese and crackers on a truly beautiful tray. My kind of snacks.

After he poured the lemonade, he sat back and looked me over speculatively. "So, what exactly is going on with you and the dragons?" Since he didn't ask it accusatively, but seemed genuinely curious, I took no offense. I explained about Dragon Enterprises, Harley's village, Pete and Doug's beer endeavors, and all the rest. He especially enjoyed hearing about Mildred's Greenpeace escapades. He had honestly thought that the videos on YouTube of her confronting whaling vessels were fakes. I offered to send him some of the videos, and he agreed.

After talking for a while, I put forth my own request. "I'd like to ask you about the wars between the dragons and the humans. I don't really want to ask my friends as they don't want to talk about it. I figured you might be more forthcoming."

He glanced over at Larry who was now watching the fish and thought for a moment. "It's a long story, but I'll give you the short version."

"Several millennia ago, humans and dragons co-existed quite well. Oh, there were occasional skirmishes when a human settlement got a bit too close to what the dragons considered their territory, but nothing radical. But as the human population grew, things started to get tense.

Well, as happens occasionally in human history, there was a lunatic named Adrien who decided that humans were the favored children of the Gods and deserved to have all the land that the dragons were keeping for themselves. He was a great orator and was quite convincing. It is said that he could impassion a crowd within just a few moments, and he spent years doing just that, traveling around the countryside railing against demon dragons.

"He managed to convince a lot of people, including several very powerful wizards, that dragons were the spawn of evil and had to be driven off of the fertile lands that the Gods had put on this earth for the use of human beings. He made it seem that the dragons were standing in the way of progress and that they were doing it at the bidding of dark forces who threatened humanity. After all, they did breathe fire, and only demons could possibly do all that. Well the wars began. Some of the wizards actually figured out how to use magic to kill dragons. After the first dragon died, the war was truly on.

"At first, it was localized. The wizards would target the dragons and the dragons would only go after those who had tried to harm them. The dragons were mostly fighting a defensive war, and they were doing pretty well. But the wizards recruited many young people who had some magical ability and taught them only one kind of magic—the kind used to kill dragons. The war escalated to the point where there were wizards in all corners of the earth going after dragons. And by then, the dragons were going after entire villages and towns.

"After several hundred years, no humans could remember a time when humans and dragons weren't at war. The dragons were a different matter.

Some of the elder dragons decided that enough was enough. They wanted to go back to a peaceful co-existence, and they decided to make this happen. They convinced most of the dragons to back off and just stay away from the humans. Things started to calm down a bit then disaster struck.

"Have you heard of the year 536?" Li asked.

"No. Can't say I'm familiar with that particular year."

"Most historians agree that it was the worst year in human history. The way it is told today is this. There was a mysterious fog, which some say was brought about by a volcanic eruption, which lasted for eighteen months. It caused the crops to fail and people to starve. On the heels of this, the bubonic plague struck, which wiped out about half the population of the Eastern Roman Empire."

"Holy crap!" I was astonished. They didn't teach us any of this in school. I looked at Li and said, "I take it that's not what really happened."

"Not even close. You see, there was one faction of the wizards that didn't want the wars to end. After all, the only magic they knew was the kind used to kill dragons. Peace would make their existence and their magic irrelevant. While the moderate wizards were pushing for peace, the lunatic fringe went into overdrive and figured out a new spell that would win the war for perpetuity. They cast a spell of the worst black magic imaginable which killed most of the wizards who participated, hundreds of dragons, and worst of all, the spell sterilized the dragons that it didn't kill."

"What?" My mind went sort of numb. I actually couldn't comprehend how anyone would wipe out an entire species and their future. But Li wasn't finished.

"Needless to say, the dragons went berserk. It wasn't a mysterious fog that blanketed the world for a year and a half, it was dragons burning everything, and I mean everything. I was extremely young at the time but was already well into my training. Thankfully I wasn't in the hands of the lunatic fringe. I found myself in the odd position of considering that the dragons had every reason to wipe out the human race while at the same time I was trying frantically to figure out how to stop them from doing so. Things were going very badly for the human race. Think of thousands of dragons burning anything they could find. The dragons very probably would have succeeded in driving us to extinction if it hadn't been for your friend over there."

"Larry?" I asked.

"Yep. He actually was *the* critical factor in ending the war. He was about twenty in the year 536, which is basically a child in terms of dragons. Since he was the last dragon that would ever be born, he had an incredible amount of power, and he decided to use it. I don't know what happened that made it his purpose in life to stop the insanity, but I am absolutely certain that if he hadn't made a move, we wouldn't be here today. He would actually fly over towns the other dragons were getting ready to take out, and put himself between the dragons and the people. Even the most mindlessly furious of the dragons wouldn't attack the youngest and possibly last dragon child to be born.

"Word of this tiny dragon who protected humans started spreading far and wide. When the tales reached the more sensible wizards, they held a conclave and decided that peace would be better than being wiped out. They reached out to the dragons and brokered a deal.

"What happened to the lunatic fringe?" I asked.

"Unfortunately, Adrien died in the spell that ended the dragon's ability to breed, so he didn't have to face his crimes. But the ones that participated in the spell and survived were turned over to the dragons. They were never heard from again. We didn't ask what the dragons did to them, and they didn't tell. After that most of the dragons left. No one knows where they went, and nobody blamed them for not wanting to stick around. The ones that remained mostly went into seclusion and slowly over the centuries they disappeared one by one."

Li stopped his tale, and I felt as if something inside of me broke. I absolutely to this day cannot comprehend how anyone could have done such a horrible thing in the name of "protecting" the human race. I was furious and devastated at the same time.

Larry rushed to my side as my anger and horror and grief continued to build. Li looked somewhat startled as I jumped on Larry's back and asked him to take me somewhere where I wouldn't have to look at another human being. I missed Li's look of contemplation as we took off.

When Larry landed, I slid off his back and crumpled to the ground. I have never before or since cried like I cried that day. Larry didn't really know what to do, so he just wrapped me in his wings and did the dragon version of "I'm here for you." Thankfully he didn't do the dragon version of "There, there." He just wrapped me a telepathic blanket of kindness. When a telepathic being is sending you soothing kindness waves, it really helps. I didn't know it at the time, but every one of my dragon friends popped in to make sure I was okay. Larry shooed them all away and told them he'd let them know what was up later.

After a long time, I took a couple of deep breaths and said, "Thanks Larry." He didn't say anything, but did open his wings. When I looked around me, I almost had a heart attack. I don't know where I expected Larry to take me, but this would not have been on the list. I was thinking somewhere in the mountains or far out on the plains or maybe even the middle of a desert. But not here. But Larry had taken me quite literally and flew me to where there was no possibility whatsoever that I would encounter another human being.

"Larry, are we on the MOON?!" I have to admit that it was a really stupid question. I could see the earth over the horizon. I could see stars like I've never seen before, and when I turned around, I could see Mars. Mars! It looked a lot brighter without all the light pollution on Earth. Bigger too.

Larry just laughed, "*Yes.*"

"How come I can breathe? No, don't answer that. I know the answer – MAGIC!" I started throwing rocks and jumping around. It was great. Better than any trampoline I've ever been on, and boy can I throw a long way on the moon. "You know, it's kind of cool up here Larry. We could build a dragon version of a treehouse. Sort of a moon-house. Then, when we need a change of pace, we could come up and have a party."

Larry just stared at me. I have to admit that it did seem like a pretty bizarre idea. But even being on the moon didn't distract me for long from what I had just learned. I got quiet again and asked Larry a question I couldn't seem to wrap my head around. "Seriously Larry, how could you guys ever forgive us? Right now I am ashamed of my entire race."

"It was a very long time ago, and it was a very small number of people. Humans have always had trouble with small groups of crazy people causing way more trouble than they should be allowed to. That's something you guys should work on. It's better but still happens way too often."

I certainly couldn't disagree with that one, and it gave me something to think about. After kicking and throwing a lot of rocks around on the moon, I had Larry take me home.

When we got back to headquarters, all of my friends were there to greet me. After reassuring them all that I was fine, we decided to break the rules and have an unscheduled movie night. I got to choose and because of my mood we watched one with lots of explosions, car chases, and dead bad guys. I needed something to distract me and having my friends, a good movie, and lot and lots of chocolate ice cream did help.

The next day I dove into work with a vengeance. I didn't really know it at the time, but I was worried about my friends. I actually had this subconscious feeling like I needed to protect them. I figured that out later. At the time I just felt a sort of unease permeating everything I did.

After several weeks I decided to put my idea of a Dragon Moon-House into effect. I grabbed a sketch pad and asked Larry to take me back to the Moon. We flew over lots of open country before I found the perfect place. It was this beautiful crater with an interesting cliff face and unique rock formations at the edge. I was thinking that it would make a great place for dragons to come in and out of—if there were openings and caves and such. I had Larry land. I sat down on a nearby moon boulder and started to sketch. Then something very odd happened. As I sketched, everything around me seemed to fade away. All my attention was centered on my sketchbook, and I drew better than I ever had before. It was very exhilarating, and I could feel a kind of light, pulsing energy coursing through me. I was completely in the zone, and my imagination was moving like an eighteen-wheeler on a downhill grade with no brakes.

Behind me Larry froze, started looking around in alarm, tasted the air, looked at me, looked at the cliffs, quietly flipped out, and then called all the other dragons. They all arrived within moments and landed behind me, per Larry's instructions, so as not to distract me. What I thought was just "being in the zone," was actually magic unlike anything any of the dragons had ever seen. As I drew, the cliffs were actually changing. When I drew a little lake and made it into a hot spring for the dragons to bathe in, it appeared and steam started curling off the surface. At that point, Larry took off to go get Li. They had been friends for a long time, and Larry was hoping Li could shed some light on what was happening. Larry thought to himself that since dragons and humans have such different magic, maybe a human could explain it.

To say Li was surprised when Larry landed at his house and demanded Li drop everything and come with him NOW, was a bit of an understatement. Li had never seen Larry quite so disturbed or quite so excited, so instead of asking for an explanation, Li jumped to Larry's back and held on. When they appeared and Li saw the entire conclave of dragons ON THE MOON, he almost fell off of Larry's back. He gasped for air he assumed wouldn't be there only to find that it was. He didn't know what astonished him more; that he was on the moon or that there were more than a dozen dragons sitting in a semi-circle behind one small human woman. He was awestruck, a little frightened, a lot curious. and absolutely amazed all at the same time. I'm probably the only person in the world who knew exactly how he felt.

They landed behind me and after sliding off of his back Li looked at Larry and asked, "What's happening, Larry?"

Larry looked at him, nodded his head toward where I sat and merely replied, *"Watch."*

It took Li only moments to see what all the dragons were watching. The landscape in front of him would glow for just a moment and then change into something else.

He turned to Larry, "Have you ever seen anything like this?"

Larry shook his head. *"No. It's magic, but it doesn't taste like any magic I've ever seen."*

"You taste magic?" Li asked.

"You don't?"

"No. I can feel it, I can even see, but taste it? No. What does it taste like?" I could have told Li that he shouldn't ask questions like that, but I was busy and wasn't even aware of the conversation.

"Magic."

Li smirked, then looked back over to where I sat. I was now sketching giant dragon size gazebos next to a nice little stream that flowed out of the hot-tub lake. As soon as I finished each sketch, I would just turn the page and start another. "How long has she been at this?"

"About three hours."

"Does she know she's using magic?"

"I don't think so. I don't even think she's really seeing it. She glances up once in a while then just keeps going."

Li looked a bit concerned, "I think we should get her to stop. She probably needs to eat something, and we don't want her to burn out the first time she uses magic. I don't know how she's gone on this long. She has to be using huge amounts of energy to pull that off."

They were on the verge of interrupting me when I stopped. I probably would have kept going, but I finally noticed that my legs had gone numb from sitting cross-legged so long. I put down my pad, stood up and stretched. I then turned around expecting to see Larry, and instead I saw all the dragons and Li. I was so startled a small yelp escaped from my mouth. "What are you guys all doing up here?"

Li took the initiative, "We were watching you create that." He pointed to the cliffs that were now behind me.

I turned and saw my vision in real-life. "Hey, that's awesome!" I turned back to all the dragons. "Did you guys do that from what I was sketching?"

Larry replied *"No."*

I turned to Li, "You did it?"

Li shook his head no.

Larry put his giant snout right up to my nose. *"You did it."*

I snorted and laughed at the same time, "Yeah right! You're funny." I slapped him on the snout much to Li's astonishment.

"You did do that."

I looked back at the cliffs. I looked at the dragons. I looked at Li. They were all nodding their heads in the affirmative. "How could I possibly have done that? I don't do magic! You guys all do magic. I'm just your friend."

No one said a thing. "I know it's not April. Is this some sort of let's-prank-Deanne day?"

Everyone shook their heads in the negative. "Well, whatever you guys are up to is fine with me. Let's go check it out!"

For the next hour or so, all of us explored the caves, played in the giant hot spring (the dragons dried me out in very gentle fire afterwards), inspected the gazebos and generally had a great time. Finally, my stomach demanded I go back to Earth to get some food. I invited Li to come back with us, and he accepted. While I was still mad at the human race, I wasn't mad at Li in particular. Besides, the dragons seemed to accept him so I figured I should as well.

Li was fascinated with Dragon Enterprises, Inc., and asked me loads of questions. He seemed particularly interested in the various jobs I had gotten for the different dragons. After he left, I got back to my normal routine.

Over the next couple of weeks, I spent quite a bit of time in Dragon Land, which is what the dragons decided to name it. The dragons made a few modifications and even brought some of their treasure to store in the caves. Every time I came up, I found something new. The day I discovered the eggs, though, was a game changer for all of us.

When Larry and I landed, I noticed there was something in the main gazebo. I wandered over only to see a number of eggs placed carefully around the floor of the gazebo. I was terribly confused so I asked Larry to clarify. "If you guys can't breed, why are there eggs?"

"All of these eggs existed before the spell was cast."

"Are there baby dragons inside?"

"We think so, but we are uncertain. We can't hear them."

"Could you before?"

"Yes."

"Wow. That seriously sucks." I wandered around through the eggs and admired the beauty of them. Each egg had a complex design in various colors. They were some of the most beautiful things I had ever seen. I turned to Larry, "Why are there so many different colors on the shells?"

Larry looked very closely at the egg closest to him. *"You see colors?"*

"Yes, and really cool designs." Larry had nothing to say. Have you ever seen a speechless dragon? It's pretty interesting. Since he didn't say anything, I asked him my next question. "Can I touch one of them?"

"Sure."

"Which one?" By this time, several more of the dragons had arrived. Apparently, they wanted to see what was going on. I still didn't buy that I had created Dragon Land, but the dragons were sure I was about to do something else amazing.

Larry pointed to one of the eggs. *"That one. We don't know whose that is."*

I walked over, looked over the egg, reached out and touched it. Immediately several things happened, none of which I anticipated. I was knocked back about twenty feet by some sort of energy surge. However, in the split second before that happened I "saw" the dragon that lay within the shell.

She was beautiful. She was a snow-white color with gold tips on her scales. I hadn't seen her eyes, but I knew for a fact that they were a brilliant emerald green. As I got to my feet a huge dragon, larger than any of my friends, appeared over our heads spouting fire and growling. I hadn't heard any of the dragons growl and was taken aback. Since he was heading for the egg, I did the only thing I could think of. I sprinted over to the egg and stood between it and the monster. I felt like the mouse in the "DEFIANCE" poster who is flipping off a diving eagle, but I just couldn't let him hurt the beautiful little dragon I had seen.

Larry then got into the spirit of the thing, jumped in front of me and folded his wings around me to protect me. I knew he could be harmed by dragon fire, so I thought him very, very brave. Because I couldn't see through Larry's wings, I didn't see that the rest of the dragons did the exact same thing. In a moment I was protected by a giant dragon-wing cocoon.

The monster of the sky stopped flaming and landed in front of where we all stood. After promising that he wouldn't harm me, the other dragons slowly stepped away and folded their wings. I imagine it looked like a huge flower blooming in time-lapse photography. Even after they released me, they stood very close while the great dragon looked me over.

"Who are you, what are you doing with my egg, and why in the world did you put your puny self in front of it when I appeared?"

I put my hands on my hips, and replied with more bravado than sense, "My name is Deanne, I was admiring it and wanted to see how it felt.

As for why I was standing in front of it, I was protecting that beautiful little dragon who is sleeping within."

"Did you actually think you could protect the egg from me?"

I was encouraged by the fact that the dragon sounded more astounded than angry. "No, I was pretty sure you were going to kill me."

"Then why did you do it?"

"Because she deserves to live."

"You saw her?"

"I did." Since his stance went from a belligerent, ready to fight attitude to one of sheer astonishment, I ventured a question of my own. "Can you tell me what these designs are?"

"What designs."

"All of the eggs have these cool colored designs on them. I was just wondering if they had a purpose."

Larry came over and intruded into the conversation. "We don't see any designs. To us the eggs just look a dull grey."

"That's terrible. Hey, if you send someone down for my paints, I'll show you what I'm talking about."

Mildred was gone and back in a flash. She had brought all kinds of paint. I chose the watercolors because I was pretty sure they wouldn't harm the egg, and had one of the dragons get me some water from the lake. I then asked the monster dragon if I could paint the egg and after assuring him that it wouldn't hurt it, he agreed. What I didn't see was Larry telling him to just shut up and let me do my thing. Larry really can be pushy at times, much to the elder dragon's surprise.

I started coloring the egg just as I saw it. As I painted the colors didn't just appear from my brush, they seemed to glow from within the egg itself as well. Once again, all the dragons appeared, settled down to watch, and held their collective breaths so to speak. As I painted the closure of the last line, I was once again blown back, but this time would have sailed much further than the twenty feet I did fly if I hadn't been caught by the big dragon's outstretched wing. "Thanks … Uh … what should I call you?"

Apparently, he'd never had a human ask his name and was trying to think of how to translate his dragon name to human words when we were interrupted by a large surge of crackling energy coming from the egg. As the energy bolts shot hundreds of feet into the air, cracks started to appear on the egg itself. Then we all saw a claw and a small spurt of flame emerge. The shell seemed to fall away, and there was the beautiful creature I had "seen" when I touched the egg.

She stretched, yawned, and looked at the crowd around her. She knew just who her father was and waddled over to him, flapping her drying wings at the same time to keep her balance. He leaned down and nuzzled her, and then all hell broke loose.

All the dragons in attendance shot into the air and performed a joyous aerial dance that just kept getting bigger as more and more dragons appeared. These were dragons I didn't know and had never seen. A couple of them looked suspiciously in my direction, so even though I wanted to stay and get to know the new addition, I decided that it was time to leave.

Even though I didn't want to drag Larry away from the dragon party, I had him take me back home to regroup and figure out what to do next. He did so, then disappeared immediately, so I guess he got to join in the party after all.

After thinking about it, I had to admit that obviously, I *could* use magic, even though I had no idea how. This being the case, I now had to figure out how to release the rest of the little dragons and then perhaps I could break the curse altogether. Just as I was contemplating what to do next, I got a call from my super-assistant Devon, "Hey boss. There is a contingent of ..." (I heard him asking a question of my visitors) "representatives from the Wizard's Council and they would like to speak with you."

"How many?"

"Five."

"Okay. Put them in conference room 3 and I'll be with them shortly. Get them refreshments."

I gave Devon a few minutes to get them settled, then walked into the room ready for anything. I noticed that Li was with them, so I nodded slightly in his direction. He merely raised his eyebrows and very slightly shook his head in a negative way. I got the message loud and clear, leave our friendship, minimal as it was, out of this. I walked over to the person who seemed to be in charge of the group and before I could speak, he blurted out, "What are you doing with the dragons?"

My mother's insistence on good manners kicked in, "Why hello. Why don't we start with introductions? My name is Deanne. And who might you be?"

Having great peripheral vision, I saw dumbfounded reactions from the other members of the group, with the exception of Li, who just smiled, almost imperceptibly, as if my reaction was exactly what he was expecting. Obviously, he knew me better than I thought.

The main man looked down his nose at me and replied, "I am Dominik Bartholomew, head of the Wizard's Council, and these are my compatriots. I am here on Council business. I repeat. What are you doing with the dragons?"

I stood and looked at him for a very long time. I have to admit that every once in a while, my Irish ancestry asserts itself. I am a full-on American, but I have the Irish abhorrence of authoritarian arrogance, and a bit of Irish temper as well. Nothing is guaranteed to get my dander up quite like someone throwing their weight around and expecting me to come to heel at the drop of a hat.

I finally spoke, "Get the hell off my property and don't come back."

"Young lady, you have no right to speak to me that way."

I just smiled and clicked the remote I had brought with me. As the roof opened, the wizards looked up to find several dragons perched on the roof of the building. The dragons had obviously caught on to the difficulty I was having and had left the party to come to my aid. Of course Larry was right there. He really does take good care of me. "Larry, would you care to escort these manner-less barbarians out of here?"

Before Larry could move, the head wizard relented. "We'll leave, but you haven't heard the last of this."

"No doubt," I replied without even trying to hide my annoyance.

Once they were gone, I asked Larry if he had some time to talk to me. The others left, and he settled down in my office.

"So Larry, where did all the other dragons come from? I thought there were only fifteen of you left."

Larry tilted his head as if listening and then answered, *"They're from other planets. When Earth became too crazy for them to stay, they found other places to live where they were welcomed."*

"That is both sad and very cool. I am glad that they found places to go. Are we talking planets in this solar system or planets out amongst the stars?"

"Both."

While I was delighted to find out that there were more dragons, I also realized that my problems were about to get worse. Suddenly we had a super-abundance of dragons (I didn't know how many more had arrived, but by the time I had left there were dozens) and we had a wizard's council that wasn't very happy about it. This looked to be the beginning of a new conflict, and I really needed to figure out a way to get the humans on this planet to embrace the dragons. In other words, I needed to make the dragons indispensable to the human race. Then, to top it off, there was the factor of getting the dragons to embrace the human race—the same one that had tried to wipe them out. Quite a dilemma.

I slept on it and thought about it over breakfast. I tried to do work, but my mind just couldn't seem to do anything more than chew on this problem. It was only when I decided to do something completely dis-related that I came up with the solution.

I've always enjoyed astronomy. I love documentaries about the planets, the stars, and space. I also love science fiction movies and books. So, in an effort to set my problem aside for a while, I turned on a movie. Halfway into the movie, I had an epiphany. All I had to do was talk the dragons into helping the human race reach the stars. I already knew they could move large objects, and they could fly to the moon in a heartbeat. They could probably move materials to the moon and perhaps even beyond, which would enable humans to colonize other places than the Earth. Then if I could figure out how to erase the curse my people had put on the dragons, maybe we could all be friends. Even as I had the thought, I found myself cynically doubting my very Pollyanna-ish hopes. But hey, it was worth doing, so I decided to just take the next step and see where it led.

I had Larry take me back up to the moon, where the celebrations were continuing. I had to find out if I could intentionally hatch the other eggs. I grabbed my paints and asked Larry which egg was his.

He sighed, "I don't have one."

"Okay, which one do you think I should try next?" I watched as all the dragons landed behind Larry. They were looking at me through hopeful eyes. I could see (and hear) that they had as many doubts as I did about my ability to duplicate my first effort. As I looked them all over, Mildred caught my eye. She looked so sad and yet so hopeful at the same time. So I asked her which egg was hers. She pointed it out to me, and I went to work.

At first, I thought the pressure to perform was going to mess me up, but luckily, I was soon so engrossed in the incredible designs that the magic flowed without effort, much as it had the first time. As I painted, I could feel my anticipation building. I couldn't wait for Mildred to see her son. He was the exact reverse of the little dragon who had hatched before him. He was coal black with scales and wings tipped in silver. This time when I was blown back, there were several dragons waiting to catch me.

When he hatched, some of the dragons wept with relief. He blinked his deep purple eyes and looked me over. My smile was so huge my cheeks were sore for the rest of the day. This was something I could do! I could bring these beautiful creatures back.

As even more dragons appeared, I asked to have a council with them. Everyone landed and surrounded me. I should have been frightened out of my wits (I mean really, one good sneeze and I would have been launched into space), but every dragon in the circle was sending me the most benign thoughts. I had never experienced anything like it.

It took me two weeks to convince the dragons that their best chance for survival as a species was to help the very species that had tried to wipe them out. My main concern, which I expressed, was that if I could create magic to bring them back, there was a distinct possibility that the magic that had decimated their ranks before could also be rediscovered. The only way to make sure we never went to war again was to become true allies and friends. Either that or they could do what they did before, and just leave Earth to us and go their merry way. I did tell them that no matter what, I would indeed continue to try to figure out how to destroy the spell that made them sterile.

It was a tough sell, but eventually they all agreed. Many of the dragons who had reappeared had a real sentimentality about Earth. They wanted to be able to come back here even if just for a visit. So after much discussion, we agreed that if I could get the humans to agree, they would help us reach the stars.

I decided to test their resolve by bringing Li up to the moon to see their reaction. I had Larry take me to Li's house once again. Larry had warned him that we were coming, so he was waiting for us by the pool.

I jumped off Larry's back and strode over to where he stood. "Hey Li. Do you want to see what I've been doing with the dragons?"

He smiled, "I do."

"Do you mind a little danger?"

He furrowed his brow. "Will it be worth it?'

"Most definitely!" I replied.

"Okay, I'm in." He jumped on Larry's back and Larry launched into the sky. Li's gasp as we arrived at the moon and the tensing of his hand on my shoulder were the only indications of his mood. The dragons all stopped what they were doing and looked our way. There was no hostility in their gaze or their thoughts, but there wasn't a lot of friendliness either. It was more than a little intimidating. Behind me Li asked in a loud whisper as he slid off Larry's back, "A LITTLE dangerous?"

"They won't hurt you, at least not today." As my feet touched the ground I pointed to where the two little dragons were playing in the lake. "Look over there and you can see what the big deal is."

I was watching Li closely. His reaction was going to tell me much of what I needed to know before I continued with my venture.

His smile was sincere as he said, "They are magnificent!" He turned to me and asked, "How did you do that?"

"I don't know. The same way I did the dragon playground here. I think I'm going to name it Intuitive Magic."

Li laughed. "That works."

The father of the first dragon I'd hatched (who had finally decided on the name Ned) came over to where we stood. I introduced him to Li, who bowed respectfully. The dragon looked him over and said, "I remember you little one. You tried to stop the wars."

Li nodded. "I wasn't very successful."

"True. But you tried, and you did change many minds, young as you were. Why did you?"

"Because you have as much right as we do to live and be happy," Li said calmly.

Ned nodded. "Good answer. Young humans seem to have a tendency to not agree with their elders if the two of you are any indication."

I laughed. "I hope that's a good thing."

Ned tilted his head. "Maybe." Then he just turned and walked away.

Li and I looked at each other. "God, I love dragons," I said, and Li smiled.

"They certainly are different. Why are there so many of them?"

"I'm not sure. When the first dragon hatched, they just started appearing. I have an idea on how to integrate the dragons and human beings. Wanna hear it?"

Li chuckled, "In for a penny." So, we went back to Dragon Enterprises and, over tea and cookies, we started brainstorming how to make this work.

I had considered reaching out to NASA, but Li pointed out that they would probably drown me in red-tape. We considered the Russian space program, but I didn't know much about it and besides, they've been being a bit weird lately. Then I thought of N-Space, the privately owned space exploration company. Li and I looked them up on the internet and found out more about their founder and their mission. These were the guys we needed to reach.

As we were 'net surfing, I found out that the founder of N-Space had launched a solar-powered car into space with a camera set up that would show you the view from the car as it drifted between the Earth and the Moon. It even had a space-suited "driver" who sat in the driver's seat with one hand on the steering wheel and his other arm on the rolled down window of the car. I loved this guy. He had my kind of insouciance. But how to get him to talk to me. Since the feed from the car was live, I had an idea.

I had my design team make me a space suit exactly like the one the dummy in the car was wearing. While they were doing that, I had Larry find the car. Outer space is a pretty vast place, but it was a fun game for him to pinpoint the location. It took us about five minutes to get to the car. I was already suited up so that it didn't take but a "jiffy," to have Larry block the cameras while I stuck the dummy in the trunk and then put myself in the driver's seat of the car.

After I buckled in, I had Larry unblock the camera and started "driving" the car. I had Larry point it at the moon and push it in that direction while I moved the steering wheel in the appropriate direction. When we reached our destination, I had him grab the back end and gently land it on the moon. I then drove it around for a while. It was a great car, and I really put it through its paces. I even jumped it off of a small rise. I couldn't believe how far it went! I had a great time! I was pretty sure that the owner of N-Space would just assume that someone was hacking the feed, so I stopped the car several times and picked up some moon rocks to put in the trunk of the car. Perfect evidence.

I then had Larry block the camera again and take the car to Mars where I repeated my antics.

I then blocked the camera one more time, and put back the original driver. I then had Larry, in the dead of night, deliver the car to the front steps of N-Space with my business card in the glove box.

The very next morning there was a message right in the middle of my desk. Sure enough it was from Eli Marshall, the owner of N-Space. He just wanted to let me know that he was on his way and would arrive at about 9:00 am. Since I'd slept in, that meant I had about thirty minutes to prepare for his arrival. I had all the dragons make themselves scarce and dashed out to Devon's desk. "Devon, I need ..."

Devon just smiled, "Relax boss, it's already taken care of. I set up a buffet in the smaller conference room. The coffee's fresh, and I set out a number of pastries, fruit, and different tea selections in case he drinks tea."

"Thank you! I don't know what I'd do without you!"

"I know. Now go back to your office, and I'll let you know when he gets here."

I did go back to my office, but the best I could do was pace. What if it didn't work? What if he just laughed at me? I tried to calm myself down by remembering that his passion in life is supposedly colonizing Mars. Well, if that turned out to be true, he was going to love my friends.

When I arrived in the conference room, he held out his hand and put me at ease immediately. "You must be Deanne. Pleased to meet you."

I smiled as I shook his hand, "Same goes. I'm a great admirer. Help yourself to some refreshments, and we'll talk."

We both got some coffee, put together small plates, and sat down at the table. He looked at me speculatively and asked, "So, how did you get my car not only to the moon but Mars, *and* then bring it back to Earth?"

I laughed. "So you're sure it's your car and not one I just made to look like it?"

"I'm sure. I had several things in the glove box that you wouldn't have known about if you'd just been trying to fake it. I take it you're the one who ate the Mars bar."

"No, actually I gave it to a friend. He said it was pretty stale. I left you the wrapper though." He chuckled as I continued. "I loved the maps in the glove box—Mars, the Moon, and the solar system. You have a warped sense of humor, sir."

"Yes, I do. So, back to my original question, how did you do it?"

I looked him straight in the eye and said, "Magic."

I can't tell you how satisfying it was to be on the other end of that answer. I've already told you how Larry had driven me crazy for years with that answer. This was the first time I had gotten to use the explanation on someone else, and I have to admit that it was really fun. The look on his face was priceless. It was a delightful combination of annoyance and disbelief. Now I get why Larry takes such pleasure in that terse explanation.

He started to say something, and I cut him off. "Just refill your coffee and I'll show you." He shrugged and did as I asked. I led him to my office, where I opened the roof. There sat Larry perched on the roof next to the opening.

Eli looked up and then took a large gulp of his coffee. He looked up again, and then looked at me. He visibly paled, but much to his credit he didn't freak out. He looked like he wanted to ask me a question, but couldn't figure out what to ask. I took pity on him and decided to explain.

"Eli, let me introduce you to Larry. He's my best friend. He's going to be our transportation for our trip today. I'm going to actually show you how I did what I did with your car. Then, I'm hoping we can work together on a project to put a colony on the Moon and then one on Mars."

My opinion of Eli rose further when he looked at Larry and said, "Nice to meet you. I'm Eli." I've never seen anyone act so calmly when first meeting a dragon.

Larry said, "*Hello,*" and then hopped into the room. Have I mentioned that my office is really big? I designed it so that the dragons could come and see me. It will fit three at a time. For larger meetings than that, we use the open-air auditorium. Eli looked at me and asked, "May I touch him?"

I nodded towards my friend. "Ask him."

He turned to Larry. "May I?"

Larry lowered his head, *"Sure."*

Eli reached out and smoothed his hand along Larry's nose. He smiled and thanked Larry. He turned back to me. "So, where are we going?"

I smiled. "The Moon."

He looked around and asked, "Where are our space suits?"

"We don't need them. Magic remember?" Eli looked doubtful, but didn't say anything.

Larry crouched down and laid his head on the carpet so I could climb up on his neck. I reached down my hand to Eli, and he joined me. "So, where would you like to go?"

Eli thought for a moment. "How about the Apollo landing site in the Sea of Tranquility?"

"I don't know where that is, but if you can get a picture of it in your mind, Larry should be able to figure it out."

In a few moments Larry said, *"Okay, I have it. Hold on."* Eli and I both did so as Larry launched into the sky.

Eli's reaction to being on the moon was worth all the trouble we had gone through thus far. He looked like a kid who just got the best Christmas present ever. He jumped a lot and reverently viewed the first flag planted on that mighty orb. After exploring a bit, he looked at me and said, "Next time we come up, we bring the car."

"Definitely."

He then asked the question I knew he was dying to ask. He walked over to where Larry was creating dust storms with his wings. "Would you be willing to take me to Mars?"

"*I would be happy to.*" Larry took us to Mars, and we did a long fly-over of some of the more interesting places. It didn't take me long to realize that Eli was already beginning to look for sites. We then went back to Earth and got down to brass tacks.

"So," Eli began, "how is this going to work?"

"I have a few ideas," I responded. "I am going to need some serious help on your end. We need to deed a portion of the moon to the dragons and get the agreement of all the world governments that this will be a binding contract. And when I say "binding," I mean it. No going back on their word, for no one or no thing. In exchange, the dragons will help get supplies and personnel up to the moon where you can build the first outpost. Then, from there we can discuss getting supplies and personnel to Mars along with what portion of that planet should be deeded to the dragons."

"You don't think small by any stretch of the imagination," Eli said.

"That's not all," I said. "We also have to make some agreements as to the dragon's presence here on Earth. Dragons don't want to own any land here with the exception of their caves, but they do want to have free access to anywhere in the world as well as having the same rights as humans"

"I see. That's going to take some doing, but I think I'm the right guy to get it done." Eli looked fiercely determined. "Let me see what I can do."

It took almost a year to get all the agreements signed and the project started. Several of the more obstreperous governments got visits from the dragons. I'm telling you, flaming dragons flying about in your skies has a tendency to change one's attitude fairly quickly—especially when rockets and missiles shot at them just explode with no damage done to the target.

Eli was astonished at how much the dragons could carry. Once the supplies were taken up, the first workers, along with Eli, went up for the groundbreaking ceremony. Although the dragons could enable everyone to breathe, it was considered a much better option to just use space suits. Eli and I decided that it would be a little too harrowing for his people to worry about whether or not the dragons would keep providing air.

It was finally time to take a little trip to the Wizard's Council headquarters. I walked in and asked to see Dominik Bartholomew. I have to say, he really didn't like me just showing up at his place any better than I did when he showed up at my place unannounced. However, I was determined to be as polite as possible, no matter how tempting it was to be as rude as he had been during our first encounter.

He came to the reception area, scowled as he noted that Larry was lounging on the lawn outside, and ushered me into a conference room. He offered me no refreshments and just looked down his rather thin nose and asked, "What do you want?"

I smiled. I couldn't help it. It takes such a tremendous effort to be that arrogant, and he looked to be truly working hard on it. "I came to answer the question you asked me a year ago."

He crossed his arms and waited for me to continue. "I'm sure you've seen some of the news coverage regarding the partnership the dragons have made with the governments of Earth. We're helping to colonize the Moon and then Mars, and then we'll figure out what we want to do from there. As to what I have been doing with the dragons, I have befriended them. I have gotten them jobs. I take vacations with them. I watch movies with them. I have helped them start businesses as well as help out villages and towns all around the world. And (I had to pause here for just a little dramatic effect), I have figured out how to hatch all the eggs that were in existence when the wizards of old cast their evil spell. I have hatched a number of them. And to top it off, I am planning to figure out how to erase the original spell so that the dragons can have children again."

He was outraged. "How dare you! Who are you to do all of these things without our permission?"

I shrugged. "Who said I needed your permission? I'm just someone who likes dragons and thinks they deserve to live too."

He sputtered, but didn't say anything more. I stood and walked to the door. I turned just before I walked out, "Maybe you should come on over to Dragon Enterprises and meet some of the dragons. They're really not what you think."

He didn't reply, so I left. He hasn't come over for a visit yet, but I think Li is working on him and the other members of the council. Maybe they'll come around. Maybe they won't. I'm going to keep trying though. In the meantime, I have more eggs to hatch, a colony to help build, and businesses to run. I tell you I'm never bored. I love my life!

CHAPTER 4

Peace

"Larry!" My vocal shout and my mental shout were both so loud that every dragon on the moon stopped what they were doing. I didn't really mean to yell that loud, but in my defense what I saw was the most incredible, unbelievable, astonishing thing I had seen in quite some time. When you're living around dragons you get astonishing every day, but this one was staggeringly astonishing.

Larry arrived instantly along with about half the dragon population of the moon. They were all very curious. Most of them had never heard me shout. The little ones pushed their way to the front as they felt this might prove to be very interesting, and they were very curious creatures. I pointed to the ground at my feet and looked at my best friend, "Larry, what in the name of all that's holy, is that?"

Larry lowered his very large head and tilted it so that his eye was right above the item I was pointing out. He raised his head, looked me right in the eye and said, *"It appears to be a dandelion."*

"That's what I thought!!! What's it doing there?"

Larry looked again, *"It appears to be growing. It is kind of pretty. I like it."*

Several of the other dragons mentioned that they too liked dandelions. I ignored them all.

"Larry, why is there a dandelion growing ON THE MOON?!"

"Because it wants to?"

I overheard one of the little dragons, I think it was Nancy, asking her mother, *"Why is she so upset about a dandelion? Doesn't she like them?"*

Ned also overheard her and answered her dryly, *"Don't worry about it little one. It's a human thing."* I swear if he could have rolled his eyes he would have.

I turned to Nancy and made a real effort to calm down. I love the little dragons and would do just about anything to not upset them. "I'm not upset Nancy, I am just surprised. Plants don't normally grow on the moon."

I overheard one of the other dragons say, *"She sure seems upset,"* as I whirled about to find the dragon who said it so I could rebut the statement, I was interrupted by Nancy.

"Flowers do so grow on the moon. I know where there are more. Would you like to see?"

"Yes. Yes, I would love to see them," I replied.

Nancy led me over to the hot spring bathing pool I had set up for the dragons and showed me all kinds of plants growing around the edge. Then she took me over to one of the gazebos and showed me even more. I stood there looking for quite a while as my thoughts whirled so quickly that I couldn't seem to grab on to one. Finally I turned to Larry, who was looking decidedly concerned. "Larry, how can this be? Why are there flowers growing all over up here?"

Before Larry could answer, Ned spoke up, *"You know, this is the trouble with you humans."*

"What do you mean?" I replied while frowning fiercely.

"You humans have to figure everything out. You can't just look at these lovely flowers and say, 'Oh how nice. There are beautiful flowers growing on the moon.' As I have listened, you have asked yourself dozens of questions regarding why they are here, how they got here, who brought them, who's been watering them, how they're getting enough sun, how they're even growing at all, and so on ad nauseam. Really it is quite annoying. It's one of your worst characteristics."

"I have to disagree," I responded rather curtly. After all he was insulting the entire human race, and I am included in that category. "Look at me. Like most humans, I don't have claws, and my teeth are really small in comparison to most of the wildlife on Earth. We're not as fast as most of the other animals on the planet, and we're definitely not stronger than anything even our own size. It is our ability to reason that has kept the human race alive at all. If we couldn't reason, we would have been eaten long, long ago and certainly would not have been able to create the civilization we did. We'd still be sitting around in caves hiding from all the frightening things that live on this planet."

Ned looked at me and thought it over. *"I will concede that point. However, you have a tendency to go overboard and to solve all the wrong problems and none of the right ones."*

I kind of felt like I should be insulted, but what Ned just said had a ring of truth, so I decided to listen instead. He continued, *"For instance, your civilization right now is all tied up and solving the problem of some people calling other people by the wrong words, when there are millions of people dying of starvation every year. You are seriously mean to each other, and some of you think you are being virtuous because you yell at people or try to destroy their businesses because they have the wrong ideas. At the same time you ignore all the people who don't even have clean water to drink. You even have inventions that can handle that, but you're so busy worrying about stupid stuff that you don't get those inventions over to all the people who need them.*

"You can't even use that impressive intellect to figure out who is crazy and who is sane, so you

marry crazy people and wonder why you aren't happy. You work for crazy people and wonder why your job isn't fulfilling. You elect crazy people to run your governments. Then those people pass laws that make your lives even more miserable, and to top it off they start wars for really foolish reasons, most of which boil down to the fact that your leaders are nuts."

Ned was right. At that moment in time, I was actually embarrassed to call the human race my own. But I couldn't go down without a little bit of a fight. "You know Ned, some of us overcome that and are really nice and do spend time and effort help others."

"True, but you should all do it. Earth could be a great place to live if you just solved the right problems," Ned replied.

"So what do you suggest Ned?"

"I suggest that you thank Nancy for showing you these lovely flowers and then figure out what problems are important enough for you to actually solve, and then get busy solving those."

I stood and looked at Ned for a long time. "You know Ned, you're right. Even though I hate to admit it, I think you're onto something. I'll try to do better." I turned to Nancy, "Thank you for showing me the beautiful flowers."

"You're welcome," she said before flying off to play with her friends.

I then turned to Ned and added, "But I am still interested in why plants are happily growing on the moon," at which point Ned just shook his head and laughed.

"Okay then. As long as you also try to think about the important things." At that point neither one of us knew just how important the plant thing was going to turn out to be.

I had Larry take me back to headquarters, and I made a list of all the important things we should be tackling. The list included things like poverty, water, international relations, etc. I then got to work on "solving" them. I looked at what we had done already, like Harley's village and Hexley's literacy project. I then researched what Ned had mentioned about inventions that can bring water to isolated areas and was astonished to see what could be accomplished. I then looked up the statistics on poverty, and was appalled at the number of people in the world who never get enough to eat, let alone have a nice house to live in.

Rather than reinvent the wheel, I found all those organizations who were successfully tackling these issue on a small scale, and then helped them garner resources to tackle them on a much, much larger scale. The dragons were a great help, and as we found even more ways to utilize their abilities, I was reminded again how much I loved my job.

But even as I worked so hard to define and tackle the "right" problems, the plants on the moon just kept eating away in the back of my mind. It just seemed that there was something I was completely missing about the whole thing. So, I reached out to the oldest and wisest person I knew – Li Chen. When Larry told him we wanted to come see him, he invited us to dinner, which sounded good to me.

We were having a lovely dinner when Li asked, "So, what is it you want to ask me about? Larry says you have something that's been driving you nuts—his words not mine."

"He's pretty much right," I said. "There's a mystery I haven't been able to even find a starting point for solving, so I thought you might be able to help me."

Larry chimed in, *"Ned thinks she thinks too much."*

Li looked at me inquisitively. "Ned is the oldest of the dragons, the one who remembered you when you were just a young wizard," I explained. "He thinks humans spend too much time spinning around in our heads solving stupid problems while ignoring the really important ones."

Li laughed, "I'm sure the next time I meet Ned, we'll have a lovely conversation. I have thought the same thing many times over." I snorted, and Li continued with an indulgent smile, "You're young. You'll see it someday."

I shrugged, "I already have. Since Ned mentioned it, I have been seeing exactly what he means and have been trying to be better."

"I see," Li said. "Now, what about this mystery? Can you give me a brief outline?"

"No, I think this is something you need to see. I don't want to give you any preconceived ideas."

So we both jumped on Larry and headed up to the moon. I had Larry land by the Gazebo, where the greatest concentration of vegetation was, and much to my surprise, the plant population had grown by leaps and bounds. There were even vines creeping up the columns of the gazebos. Li jumped off of Larry's back and strode over to the plants. He looked, he touched, he picked off a flower and smelled it, and then just looked at me with the strangest look on his face. "You know, it's been several hundred years since I've been completely astounded, but this—this is great. There are plants growing on the moon. That's the best thing I've seen in years!"

Li spent the next few minutes just exploring the different types of plants and flowers and exclaiming when he found a rare or particularly interesting one.

Ned quietly landed behind me and nudged me in the back, *"See, that's what I'm talking about. This man understands how important it is to see the joy."*

I just laughed and smacked him on the nose. "Okay, okay, okay—point made. Enough already!"

Li looked up from the plant he was studying, "Did you just smack that behemoth on the nose?"

"Yeah."

"I have never in all my years met anyone like you."

Ned looked over at Li, *"Neither have we. She's very disrespectful."*

"No, I'm not! I'm just precocious. I am only in my second decade, while the two of you are … well, you're not."

Li looked at Ned. "Did she just call us old?"

Ned narrowed his eyes, *"I think she did. But she managed to not make it sound like an insult. Perhaps she does respect her elders."*

I smiled, "Yeah, you two just keep thinking that." They both laughed. I have great friends. Hmmm, I hadn't really thought of Li as a friend before. Maybe I needed to change that and spend more time with him. He is a really good guy.

After Li inspected all the plants, he and I went back to his house to figure out what we needed to figure out.

Over dessert we talked about magic in general. I found it fascinating since I knew so little about how magic worked. Li knew that the plants had to do with magic, but neither one of us could figure out how. It was a brainstorming session that went something like this.

"So Li, how can magic affect life itself."

"How can it not?"

"I looked at him quizzically, "What do you mean?"

"Well let's start with you. No one has taught you any magic, but by just being around the dragons, you started using it."

"Hmmm," I replied. So are you suggesting that by hanging around with magical creatures, we might be able to become magical ourselves?"

"I don't honestly know. It has never actually crossed my mind." Li replied. "In the past we have always just looked for people who showed magical ability, and we then apprenticed them in its use. We never considered why they were magical."

"Interesting." I said. "When you were talking to me about the wars, it seemed that there were loads of wizards as well as wizard apprentices. Is that correct?"

"Yes."

"And how many are there now?"

Li thought it over. "Well we have a core group of the elders, which means those who have been around more than a thousand years, and that is about twenty wizards."

"Really? What happened to all the others? I thought there were quite a few."

"There were, but over the years they have slowly died off. Some of them had accidents, some just passed away from old age."

"And what about younger wizards?"

"We have about a hundred of those. But they are getting harder and harder to find."

"Hmmm. I have another question. Where did you find the last few wizard apprentices?"

"We just found one in the Caribbean on a little island named Bonaire. And before that, the last one we found was in China."

I just looked at Li and shook my head slowly. "That is very interesting."

Li looked at me suspiciously, "Why?"

"Because Hexley, the first dragon I ever met, has been living in the Caribbean on a little island named Bonaire since I was a teenager. He often has the children read him stories."

"Are you suggesting that the dragons are the source of our magic?"

"I'm not suggesting a thing. I am merely pointing out an interesting fact. If we take this as a hypothesis, we can do some further research and see if it holds up."

And that is exactly what we did. With the dragons' help, we made a historical map of where the dragons used to live and where they live now. Li then put together a spreadsheet of all the members of the Wizard's Guild including where they lived, when they were first discovered, and the date of their discovery as a wizard. The data was fascinating. Every wizard now alive was living near where a dragon lived when they were "discovered".

We then took a little trip to Harley's village, where Li did some testing of the local people. He found several that had some magical ability. Then we went to the places where no dragons had lived for over a thousand years and found that not only was there no trace of magical ability, those places were also lacking in flora and fauna.

Suddenly our theory expanded. Could it be that magic was somehow involved in life itself? We still haven't fully committed ourselves to saying it is, but the evidence certainly seems to point that way.

We did determine that that magic sort of leaks from the dragons to their surroundings, thus gracing everything around them, including humans, who then become somewhat magical themselves.

We then made the discovery that tied it all up in a bow for us. We listed out all the wizards who had died over the last five hundred years and compared that to the locations the dragons lived. None of the wizards that had passed on had lived anywhere near a dragon at the time of their death. Most of the wizards still alive had dragons living in their vicinity, even though they were unaware of it.

Li and I agreed that we needed to give this info to the Wizard's Council, but we both knew that they wouldn't accept it easily. So I hired a marketing firm to help me put together a really nice PowerPoint presentation to help them accept it. Since I was not in good odor with Dominick Bartholomew, the head of the council, we decided that Li should do the presentation and I would accompany him, as I was the one who knew the dragons best.

The day of the presentation arrived. Li had arranged for a projector to be part of our meeting, and I was to be the AV person. When we walked in Li was greeted graciously (after all he is the oldest living wizard) and I was greeted with barely suppressed resentment and several hard glares. I was expecting nothing else.

Bartholomew spoke first, "I can't believe you are associating with the likes of her."

Li, calm as Confucius replied, "You will soon find out why."

I set up my laptop, hooked it up to the projector, and we were off and running. Having Li do the presentation enabled me to watch the various wizards to see how our presentation was going. As the maps and graphs and other information was presented, I could see the attendees change from suspicious disbelief, to curiosity, and then to a cautious acceptance. The only one who seemed determined to disbelieve it all was Bartholomew. He remained steadfastly close-minded.

When Li finished, Bartholomew went off, "Li you are a traitor to your own kind. She," he fairly spat out the word, "has poisoned your mind, and you have fallen for it."

Before Li could respond my Irish kicked in once again. I don't know what it is about Bartholomew, but he has an uncanny ability to get me really furious in a very short span of time. I strode toward Bartholomew with my righteous indignation rising. "Why you officious jerk. You wouldn't know the truth if it jumped up and slapped you in the face. How could you look at all this data and just reject it out of hand? How could you impugn the integrity of a man you have known for hundreds of years? Have you no curiosity? Have you no brains? Have you no ability to think? I swear I have met four-year-olds with more power to reason than you."

Bartholomew jumped to his feet and before anyone could react, he made some sort of hand gesture in my direction and sparks literally flew from his fingertips. They zoomed toward me but as they approached my space, they broke like a wave on a rock and sailed around me. They packed some power because when the spark waves hit the wall, it cracked dramatically.

Everyone in the room, except Bartholomew, took a step back. I looked at the wall and then back at the mad wizard. "Did you just try to harm me?" If my temper was up before, it was now in full orbit. I didn't notice it, but everyone else in the room could feel the magic building like a tsunami around me. Li took a step forward to intervene, and I just said, "Don't."

He stopped and everyone waited to see what I was going to do.

I stepped forward towards Bartholomew and was pleased to see that finally something had broken through his arrogance. He stepped back, and I finally felt the power coursing through me. So did all my friends who dropped what they were doing to come to my aid. Li said afterwards that all the wizards watched through the large windows in the conference room as dozens of dragons landed on the lawn. Everyone waited.

I was pretty confident in that moment, that if I unleashed the power that had built around me on Bartholomew, he wouldn't have a chance. I also knew that because of my inexperience with magic, I couldn't control how much I hit him with, and it might just be fatal. And no matter how satisfying it might be to get my revenge on this bully, I wasn't prepared to destroy him. That was something I would never be able to take back and would have to live with for the rest of my life. Even in my fury, I also didn't think he deserved death for being a jerk. So through a serious effort, I calmed myself and pointed at

Bartholomew "You are an idiot, and you need to resign right now."

"Never," he spat.

I turned to the others in the room. "Then you guys need to fire him."

One of the wizards spoke up immediately, "I move that Dominick Bartholomew be removed as the head of the Wizard's Council."

The motion was seconded and unanimously carried.

"You can't do this." Bartholomew demanded.

"I'm pretty sure they just did." I replied. "Now, you need to go somewhere where my friends and I won't be bothered by you anymore."

"You don't have the power. You can't keep me away."

I just looked at him and smiled. Intuitive magic is a fascinating thing. As soon as I had noticed the power building, I knew exactly how to use it and although my temper had calmed, the magic I had built up was still there. I smiled a very wicked smile and after checking to ensure no one was near it, I disintegrated the large wizard statue in the roundabout at the front of the building. I made sure it was loud and spectacular, but the show didn't harm anyone. The dragons roared their approval and added fire to the mix, melting the pile of metal shards I had created into a big pile of slag.

I then looked at Bartholomew and raised my eyebrows. He raised his hands in front of him in a gesture of surrender, and without another word, he left.

I turned to look at the stunned wizards who were staring at me. One of them ventured, "So what now?"

"I suggest you elect a new Head Wizard and get on with it."

One of them looked at me and timidly asked, "Would you—?"

"Absolutely not," I replied. "I already have too much to do."

They then looked at Li and before they could even ask the question of him he said, "Don't look at me. I'm not interested."

And with that, Li headed for the door, and I grabbed my laptop and followed him. As we exited the building I glanced his way, "You don't want to help them reorganize?"

"Heavens no. I hate paperwork."

I just laughed. A kindred spirit indeed.

Several weeks later I got an invite from the newly reorganized Wizards Council. Li, Larry and I, as well as any other dragons who were interested, were invited to a party at the Council headquarters. I graciously accepted as did Li, Larry, and a number of the other dragons. I think some of them came just to make sure it wasn't a trap.

We arrived right on time and were pleased to see live musicians, dancers, food, and all kinds of other entertainment. After Larry sent a message to the other dragons that it was truly a party, many of them came as well. They enjoyed themselves immensely. and I had a pretty good time myself..

About mid-way through the celebration, the new head wizard, Shaun Crawford, came over to where I stood.

"I wanted to ask you a favor," he ventured.

"Okay, shoot."

"I have to confess that I had an ulterior motive for throwing this party. We would like to broker a peace with the dragons. We would also like to see if we can figure out how to remove the spell our ancestors cast that ended their ability to procreate."

Every dragon in the place overheard. I didn't know it until then, but the dragons were still very suspicious, so they were keeping a very close eye on me and listening in on all my conversations. They all stopped what they were doing, and Ned sailed over to where we were standing. Since he was the oldest dragon, he had become the informal spokesman for the group.

"If you help us, there will be peace between us forever," Ned offered with all sincerity.

Shaun looked up at Ned and nodded. "So be it. I think we need to get to work."

Over the next few months the wizards and the dragons could be seen together often. Sometimes wizards were on the moon and sometimes dragons were at the wizard headquarters. But the person who figured it out was Tim, the youngest wizard from Bonaire.

He had just arrived on the moon, and one of the young dragons rushed over to see him. Have I told you that baby dragons are dangerous? They're big and clumsy, and their little scales are really hard and sharp after about three months. Well in his rush to greet his friend, Charlie, the baby dragon, misjudged his landing and sent Tim flying. This was a fairly usual occurrence, but this time Tim hit his head on a rock and didn't get up right away.

Charlie screamed and dragons rushed over to see what was happening. Ned was the first one to reach Tim, and he nudged him gently with his snout to see if he was okay. As he was doing so, he evidently checked him telepathically as well.

As Ned announced to all that Tim was fine, Tim opened his eyes and gasped. I had just arrived and was checking his head to make sure there wasn't any major damage (which there wasn't) when Tim looked at me and said, "Hey, I saw something. It might be important."

"What kind of a something?"

"When Ned was checking to see if I was all right, I saw something dark in his head. Sort of a dark swirling mist. It was weird."

I turned to Ned, "Can you do to me what you did to Tim, so I can see what he is talking about?"

"Sure." Ned did so, and other than a pretty wide-open channel, I "saw" nothing.

I turned to Larry, "Can you please go get Li?"

Larry leapt into the sky and disappeared.

As we were waiting, I overheard Charlie's mom giving him a gentle dressing down for hurting Tim. She explained that humans are fragile, soft, squishy, and easily broken, and one must take care to not harm them when one is playing with them. Charlie was appropriately contrite and went off explain his new lesson to his friends. I chuckled. It reminded me of the lecture my mom gave my little brother when we first got a puppy.

When Li arrived, I explained what had happened, and he, too, "looked" into Ned's head. He saw nothing as well. Then, with Ned's permission, I had Tim look again and see if he could remove the cloud. He tried and while his efforts lightened the mass up a bit, he couldn't get it to go away.

Ned however, was completely intrigued. As Tim had tried his magic, Ned was getting interesting flashes. He had been facing the gazebo, and for just a moment he had seen the beautiful designs on the shells from the hatched dragons. Up to this point I was still the only one who could see them. Even though they had returned to their usual grey in his perception, Ned was ecstatic. It did seem that we had discovered the magic that was blocking them.

I had Tim check to see if he could see that same swirling cloud in the other dragons and he could. Unfortunately, even the newly hatched dragons had this in their heads.

We then had a giant meeting between all the dragons and all the wizards. We had to hold it on the moon, as we didn't have a location large enough for all of us on earth.

We explained to all the wizards what had happened and had a number of them check to see if they too could perceive what Tim could. None of them could. I looked at Tim and said, "It looks like it will be up to you." I then chuckled and added, "No pressure!"

While I was joking, Tim just looked a little panicked. Li looked at the other wizards, "How about we just give Tim's magic a boost by adding our power to his?"

Shaun looked at him and said, "That would probably work. Let's try it with a few and see how it goes."

We all agreed. I then chimed in. "Should we send the other dragons away so that if this goes awry they will still be okay?"

The dragons protested and argued, then decided that the parents would take their babies away, but whomever else wanted to stay could do so. No other dragon left.

We chose which wizards would be the battery for Tim's magic, and after Li explained to all of us how to push our power to another, Tim wrapped his arms around Ned's snout and laid his head on it as well. The wizards then conjured magic, and bit by bit, slowly, cautiously, fed it over to Tim.

It wasn't dramatic. The magic created no fireworks, trumpets didn't sound, but after a few minutes Tim dropped his arms and turned to us. We sincerely thought he was going to tell us that it didn't work when Ned let out a dragon-sized sigh of relief and just said, *"It worked. Whatever it was is gone. I feel whole again."*

Then there were fireworks, trumpets, and all the rest. The dragons went nuts in a celebration that made the earlier one when I hatched the first dragon pale by comparison. In fact we made so much hullabaloo that several people from the newly completed moon base came over to see what all the fuss was. We invited them join in on the celebration, and they did. They loved the fact that they could take their space suits off and run around the moon. Everyone had a great time.

Ned found a lady friend, and after several months, a new dragon egg was laid. It was the first egg laid in over a thousand years. Everyone could now see the beautiful designs on the shell, and the new baby's hatching was the most well-attended ever, by dragons, humans, and wizards.

Needless to say, Tim has become the most popular wizard in the galaxy. He's certainly got his work cut out for him because new dragons are arriving every day from every corner of the Galaxy to get repaired. I am delighted that someone else can help with the re-establishment of dragons. For so long it was all up to me. But all the other wizards are all contributing, and peace has finally come between our two species.

At the hatching Li and I were watching the proceedings. We were both feeling pretty self-satisfied when something flitted by my face. I looked at Li, "Was that a fairy???"

The End

(or maybe not)

Glossary

a sight to behold: an amazing or wonderful thing to see

abated: become less strong, lessen

acoustics: the quality of a location that affects how you hear sounds; for example it can make sounds more clear or make them carry farther

acquiescence: agreeing to something someone else wants even if you don't really agree with it

ad naseum: doing something over and over to the point where it is so boring or annoying (or almost makes you sick)

adverse: in a bad way; affecting you badly

affirmative, in the affirmative: a fancy way of saying "Yes"; agreeing to something

Amphitheater: a large open area surrounded by rows of seats sloping upward

ancestry: people related to you that lived a long time ago and includes where they lived

anticipated: expecting that it would happen; waiting for something exciting to happen

antiquities: valuable old things from long ago, like pirate treasure, old coins, old pots, etc.

appalled: shocked because something is so bad

approached: to move closer to someone or something

arrogance: being too self-important and treating others as though they aren't

aspiring: someone who wants to be something but hasn't made it yet

asserts: to demonstrate that something is there; example - if your anger asserts itself, it means it comes out in a way that is easy to see

assess: to consider something carefully so as to get information about it or make a decision about it

assure: to make someone more certain of something

Glossary

barraged: to direct a large number of something at someone; example, "He was barraged by questions" means he was asked many questions very quickly

belligerent: to be hostile or angry

bemoan: to complain about

benign: kind, gentle and harmless

berserk: crazy and out of control

bidding (at the bidding of): at someone else's request; doing what someone else wants you to do

binding: you absolutely have to follow it - it can't be broken

bogus: not real, not true, fake

brass tacks, get down to brass tacks: to get to work on the details and realities of something

bravado: looking and acting like you are brave

brokered: to arrange an agreement with two groups or two people

broody: thinking about something a lot in an unhappy way

butterfly net: a lightweight, fine net on the end of a pole used for catching butterflies

cacophony: a loud unpleasant mixture of sounds

CG: Computer Generated—refers to images and movie parts that are made on a computer rather than filmed in real life

compatriots: the people that one works with or hangs around with

conclave: a private meeting

contemplated: to think about something carefully for a long time

contrite: very sorry because you have done something wrong

controversial: something that people disagree with and often argue about

convenient: very easy or useful

Craig's list: an online place to go to find goods for sale or jobs

crestfallen: sad or disappointed about something

cryptic: containing a hidden meaning that is hard to understand

curtly: speaking in a rather short and rude way

Glossary

cynical: believing the worst of people; believing that people care only about themselves and are not sincere or honest

dander (get one's dander up): to become or to cause someone to become annoyed or angry

decidedly: without a doubt: very much

decimated: to spoil or destroy something

determine: to figure out or to decide

devastated: 1. completely damaged or destroyed. 2. feeling very shocked and upset

diagnostic: used for finding out what is wrong with a piece of equipment

dilemma: a situation in which you have to make a difficult decision

disputes: arguments or disagreements

divested: to take off what you are wearing or carrying

downside: the part of something that is less pleasant

drama queen: someone who reacts to situations in an exaggerated or dramatic way

dutifully: carefully or obediently doing what is expected or what you should do

eloquently: learly expressing something

emphatically: in a forceful way that leaves no doubt

employers: people who give one jobs

enigmatic: mysterioius and difficult to understand

ennui: a feeling of being bored and having no interest in anything - pronounced on-we

epiphany: a sudden realization or understanding of something important

epitome: the best possible example of something

escalated: to make a bad situation worse

exhilarating: something that makes you feel excited and very happy

expectantly: excited because you think something interesting is about to happen

extrapolation: to take information you have and made a good guess based on that information about something else

Glossary

facetious: saying something you don't really mean in an attempt to be funny

faction: a particular group; a clique

fantastical: something that exists in your imagination and might not be real

flaps: a movable part of an airplane wing that causes it to go up and down

flora and fauna: plants and animals

foothills: a series of low hills at the base of the mountains

forthcoming: willing to give information when asked

fortunately: showing that something's a good thing

freakishly: awesome because it is not normal

funny farm: a mental hospital

gamut: the complete range of something - all of it

garner: to collect or gather up

geothermal: heat that is produced by the earth like volcanos or hot springs

Dragons, Inc.

get your tail in a twist: to become upset or worried or upset about something, from the phrase to get your panties in a twist (which would make you upset)

gist: the general idea of something

Grand Ole Opry House: a concert hall in Nashville Tennesee which is famous for its country music concerts

hallucinations: things you see that aren't really there.

harrowing: extremely upsetting or disturbing

hoax: a prank or a trick of some sort

HR: Human Resources - the part of a company that is in charge of the people that work there

huff (in a huff): acting badly because you are annoyed and offended

humongous: very large or very important

hydraulic fluid: a fluid, usually thick, used in various machines

hypothesis: an idea that attempts to explain something but has not yet been tested or proved

Glossary

imperceptibly: so slight or small that it is very difficult to notice

impugn: to say that someone does not deserve to be trusted or respected

in the trenches: actively doing something rather than just watching

incredulous: finding something very hard to believe

indignation: anger you feel because something is unfair

indispensable: you can't do without it

indulgent: treating a person with special kindness even if it is sometimes not good for them

inevitable: it is certain to happen and cannot be prevented or avoided

infrastructure: basic things that are needed such as transport, communications, power supplies, and buildings, which enable a community or country to function.

insouciance: not being too serious about things, feeling cheerful like nothing is bothering you

Dragons, Inc.

inspiration: a sudden feeling of enthusiasm, or a new idea that helps you to do or create something

instantaneously: without any time going by, right now

integrate: to combine two things successfully

intestinal fortitude: courage or guts

intimidating: frightening in a way that makes people lose confidence

Intrigued: very interested

intriguing: very interesting or strange

intruded: to go somewhere even when you aren't invited

intuitive: to feel that it is true although you have no evidence or proof

iridescent: showing changing colors in different types of light

Irish (one's Irish comes out: to become or cause to become angry, hostile, defensive, or irritable

justification: reasons you give for why you did something often something bad

Glossary

lead (lead guy): the person who is skilled at some job and so is in charge of others at that same job

majestically: done in a way you think is beautiful and impressive like something a king or queen would do

mayhem: some thing or some action that is disorganized, confused, and often violent

meantime: the time between one thing and another

melodrama: a story or play in which there are a lot of exciting or sad events and in which people's emotions are overdone

mellowest: most kind, gentle, relaxed and cheerful

millennia: periods of 1,000 years

miscreants: someone who has behaved badly or done something against the law

mode: the manner in which one does something

mull over: a fancy way to say you are thinking something over

mundane: ordinary and not very interesting

mystifying: finding something impossible to explain or understand

naïve: not having much experience and so expecting things to be easy or people to be honest or kind

navigate: to move carefully in order to avoid hitting things or hurting yourself

Nessie: a creature in Scottish tales that is said to live in a lake (Loch Ness) in Scotland

nestled: put in a place that is comfortable and safe like a nest

nonetheless: despite what you just said, you're now going to say something else that might be different

obstreperous: refusing to behave in a sensible way and sometimes protesting loudly

odor, in good odor: to be well thought of by someone

old hands: people who have been there and done that; experienced people

onset: when something starts

optimist: someone who always looks on the positive side of things

Glossary

orator: someone who is very good at speaking in public and getting people to listen

penny (in for a penny): a shortening of the phrase "in for a penny, in for a pound" which means that since you started it you're going to finish it.

peripheral vision: what is seen at the side of your vision when looking straight ahead.

permeate: to spread throughout something

perpetuity in perpetuity: it will last forever

pinpoint: to find where something is exactly

pluck: determined courage

poker face: the ability to not change expression so people you are playing cards with don't know if you have a good hand or a bad one

Pollyanna: a character in a movie who always thought the best of people no matter what

preconceived: forming an idea or opinion before having the evidence for its truth or usefulness

prop guys: people on a movie set who care for props which are objects that an actor interacts with in a film

provoke: to deliberately try to make someone angry

psychic: having a mysterious power that lets someone know what other people are thinking, or what is going to happen to them

puttering around: to spend time in a relaxed way doing small jobs and other things that are not very important

quaint: attractive because it is unusual and old-fashioned

quizzically: in a way that shows that you are surprised or amused by their behavior

rabid: expressing your opinions in a very strong way, or behaving in an unreasonable way in order to make a change

rail against: To protest, criticize, or complain angrily about someone or something

reassured: to make someone feel less worried about something

rectified: to correct a problem or mistake, or to make a bad situation better

regard (in high regard): to think well of someone to respect and admire them

166

Glossary

renaissance: a period of European cultural, artistic, political and economic "rebirth" following the Middle Ages

renaissance festival: an outdoor weekend gathering open to the public which tries to recreate the times of the Renaissance for the amusement of its guests

reprobates: someone who behaves in a way that you do not approve of

resolve: to solve a problem, or to find a satisfactory way of dealing with a disagreement

sandstone: a type of rock made from layers of sand that have become hard over many years

sarcasm: saying or writing the opposite of what you mean

seclusion: being in in a quiet place away from other people

sentimentality: having a tender or affectionate feeling towards something

sincerely: really or honestly

skeptical: having doubts about something that other people think is true or right

smirk: to smile in an annoying self-satisfied way

sobbed: to cry so hard that you have to gasp for air

sofa tubers: couch potatoes - people who spend too much time on their couches watching TV

spawn: the children or eggs of something, offspring

sported: to wear openly and without any shyness

speculatively: in a way that shows that you are thinking hard about something

steadfastly: in a way that is firm and unwavering

sterilize: to make it so that one cannot have children

structure: how something is put together or the parts that put it together

suffice: it will do well enough, even though it might not be the original thing you wanted

sufficiently: it is enough

super-abundance: abundance - a lot of something; super-abundance - a huge amount of something

sustained: to suffer or experience, especially damage or loss

Glossary

take someone down a notch: to reduce or damage one's ego or pride: to humble or humiliate someone

terse: brief and sometimes annoyed or unfriendly

testy: easy to make impatient, annoyed or angry

the roadrunner: a cartoon where a coyote is always trying to catch a bird called a roadrunner who is so fast he leaves dust behind him

theoretically: something might be true, but you're not totally sure it is; existing in your mind as an idea

thriving: very successful

thug: a man who is violent, especially a criminal

tirade: a long angry speech criticizing someone or something

to boot: in addition to something else

uncanny: not normal or expected and a little bit mysterious like maybe it is magical

underlying: on the bottom of something or under its surface

unease: a feeling of not being comfortable about something, being nervous or not happy

unsavory: unpleasant or unacceptable

unsettling: it makes you feel rather worried or uncertain

utilize: to use

vantage point: the place from where you look at something

vat: a large barrel or tank in which liquids can be stored.

vast: a huge amount of something or and area that is very large

vengance (with a vengance): it happens to a greater extent than was expected

ventured: to do something even if it might be dangerous

wannabe: a person who tries to be something

waylay: to interrupt someone to have a conversation with them

whaler: someone who hunts whales for a living

whatsoever: used to emphasize that something is not going to happen

Glossary

whoever: which person out of all the people you are talking about

wingspan: how wide end to end and bird's wings or an airplane's wings are (or a dragon's wings)

wrangler: in movies, a person who is responsible for animals, small children, etc.

wryly: showing dry humor or finding something funny, but not in a laugh out loud way

zen master: used to refer to an individual who teaches Zen Buddhist meditation and practices, usually implying longtime study and subsequent authorization to teach and transmit the tradition themselves